dauid orme

has written too many books to count, ranging from poetry to non-fiction.

When he is not writing he travels around the UK, giving performances and running writing workshops.

David is a huge science fiction fan and has the biggest collection of science fiction magazines that the Starchasers have ever seen.

starchasers

the galactic shopping mall

by

dauid orme

illustrated by
jorge mongiovi

Ransom

starchasers

The Galactic Shopping Mall
by David Orme

Illustrated by Jorge Mongiovi

Published by Ransom Publishing Ltd.
51 Southgate Street, Winchester, Hants. SO23 9EH, UK

www.ransom.co.uk

ISBN 978 184167 764 4

First published in 2009

A CIP catalogue record of this book is available from the British Library.

DATA FILE

misha hanson
captain

- Owner of the *Lightspinner*.

- When her rich father died, Misha could have lived in luxury – but that was much too boring.

- She spent all the money on the *Lightspinner* – and a life of adventure!

- Misha is the boss – but she doesn't always get her own way.

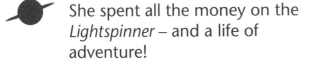

"Whenever we're in trouble, I know I've got a great team with me. The Starchasers will never let me down!"

DATA FILE

SUMA

SCIENCE OFFICER

He may look like a cat from Earth, but he is an alien with a brilliant mind for science – and sharp teeth and claws!

Probably the smartest cat in space. Finn and Misha don't need to tell him that – he knows!

Suma's not always easy to get on with. Take care – he makes a dangerous enemy!

"Misha tells people I'm just a big softy. The biggest softy in the galaxy. You know what? She's wrong."

DATA FILE

finn
2021

pilot

- Finn is a great guy to have around when there's trouble – and for the Starchasers, that's most of the time.

- Probably the best pilot Planet Earth has ever produced – though Misha and Suma don't tell him that, of course!

- Finn is great for getting the Starchasers out of (and sometimes in to) trouble! If only he didn't love gadgets so much …

"I was in big trouble when Misha found me in an on-line computer game. She changed my life!"

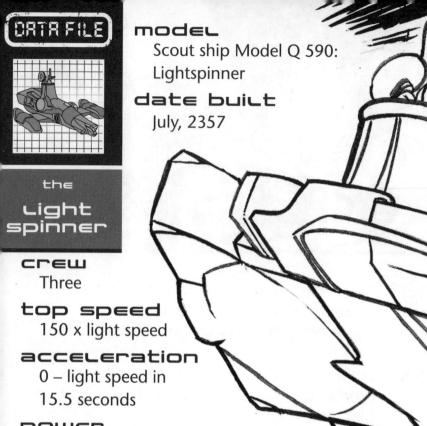

DATA FILE

model
Scout ship Model Q 590:
Lightspinner

date built
July, 2357

the
Light spinner

crew
Three

top speed
150 x light speed

acceleration
0 – light speed in
15.5 seconds

power
Faster than light – 2 Quantum Engines
Sub light speed – 2 Fermium Thrusters

Landing craft
1 x Model LC250 Lander

communication
Spacenet™ multiphase

navigation system
R.O.B 57 series computer

*"THE TOP-OF-THE-RANGE SOUND
SYSTEM WILL BLOW YOUR MIND!"*

SPACE SOUNDS   APRIL 2357

"THE NEW Q590 – LIGHT SPEED IN 15.5 SECONDS – YOU'RE GONNA LOVE THIS BABY!"
WHAT SPACESHIP JANUARY 2557

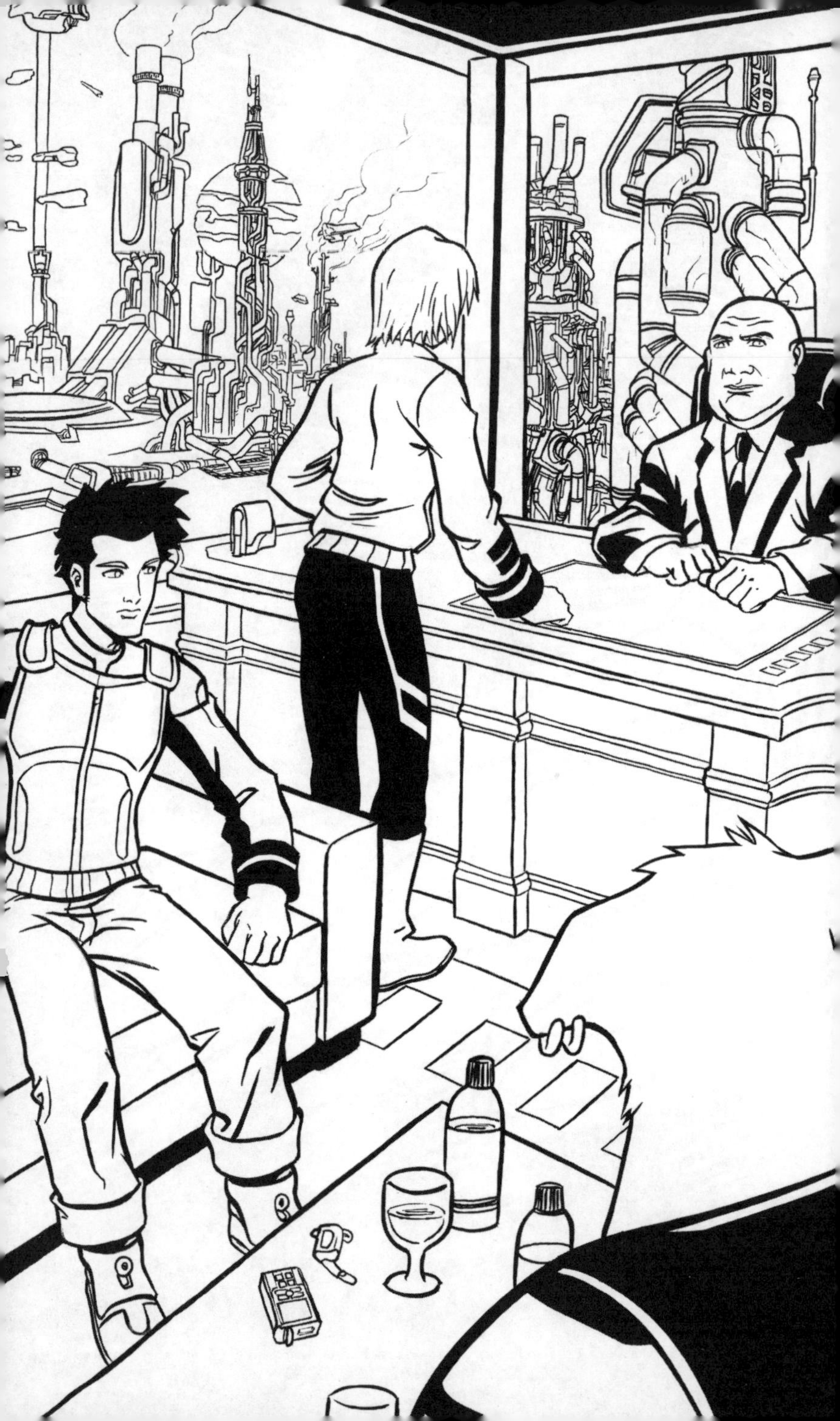

robocom inc.

The Starchasers had never been in an office as grand as this. Outside the window, the Robocom factory stretched for miles. Everything was huge – especially the boss, Ripp Gunn.

'So let's get this straight,' said Misha. 'You had a row with Ella, and now she's gone, and you'll pay us good money to find her?'

'That's right. Misha, you and Ella went to school together; she'll listen to you. It's vital that she comes back home soon.'

'Not sure it's any of our business,' said Finn. 'If Ella wants to go away for a while, surely that's up to her.'

'Yes, you're right, of course. But there's something else. I'm an old man, and I'm dying. Doctors tell me that in a couple of months I'll be dead. Ella's a good engineer and will take over the business. But I want to see her – talk to her – before it happens.'

'So what was the quarrel about?' asked Suma.

'I'm sorry, I can't tell you that.'

'Have you any idea where we should start looking?' asked Misha.

'Yes. I know exactly what planet she is on. And I'm afraid she is in great danger. She is on Trajan!'

trajan

'Trajan control. Identify.'

'Spaceship Lightspinner, with three crew.'

'Checking credit.'

There was silence for a few seconds.

'Credit O.K. Landing bay 59 – left.'

Misha and Suma looked down on to the planet's surface. It didn't look anything

special; mostly green fields growing food, with a food factory here and there, and eight spaceports scattered across the planet.

Finn smiled. There was much more to Trajan than you could see from space. The dangerous bit was underground.

It had all started a hundred years ago. A rich property dealer had bought land on the planet. He had a plan – to build the greatest shopping mall in the galaxy!

The shopping mall was a huge success. The galaxy was big, and many people earned lots of money. And people love shopping!

But people wanted choice, and soon more shopping malls appeared on Trajan. Because the weather was not good, the shopping malls were built underground.

More people came, and the shopping malls got bigger and bigger. Soon, the whole planet was nothing but tunnels, express railways, hotels, and of course, shops. Millions of them, all underground. People came for a shopping holiday and spent lots of money. Sometimes they just never went home.

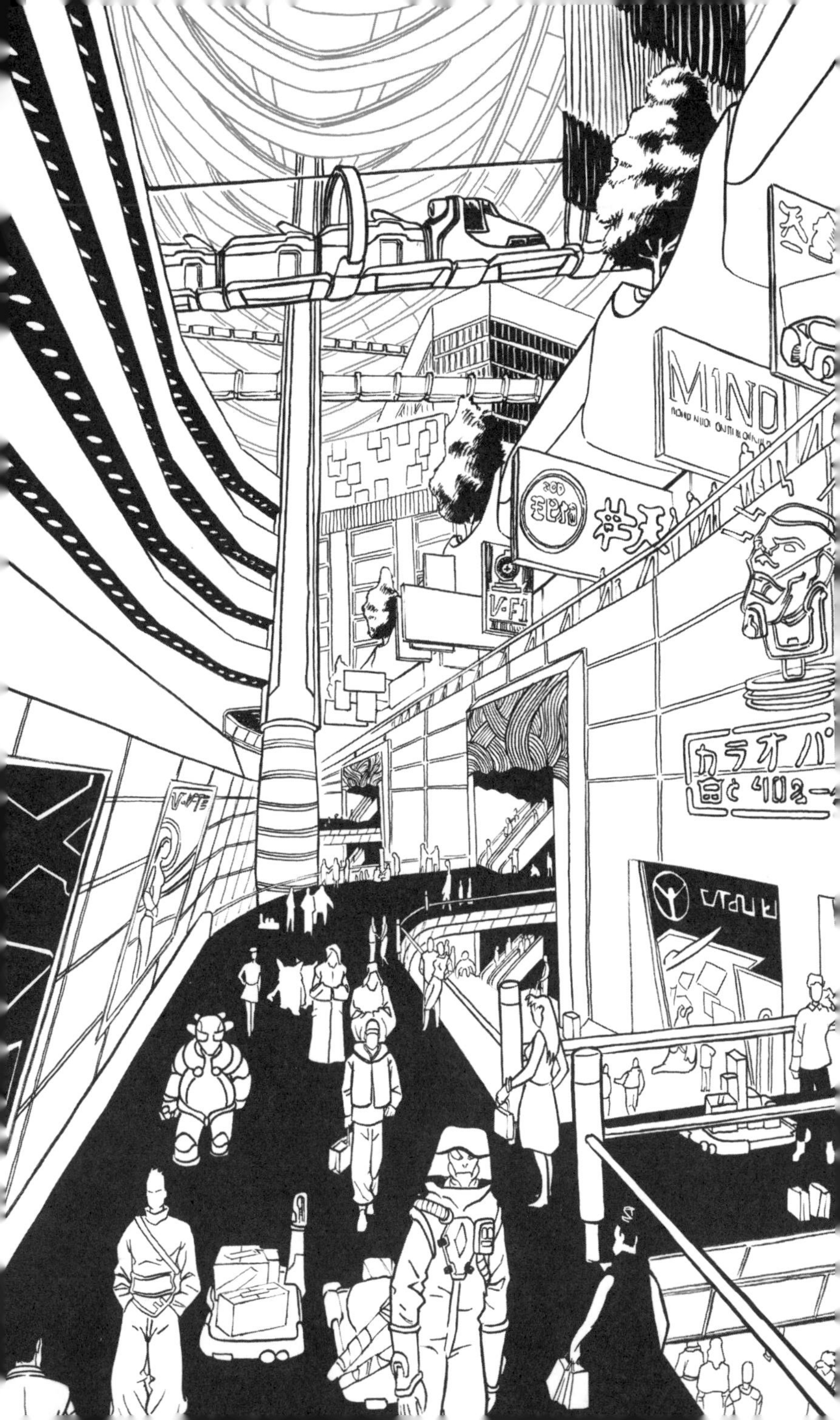
MIND
V-F1
カラオパ

Finn had been to Trajan before, when he was younger. He hadn't meant to spend much – he just wanted to look. But it had taken years to pay off his credit debts. So before they landed, Misha made a rule for the team.

No shopping!

Ripp Gunn knew Ella was on Trajan because her shopping bills were coming to him! Of course, Ripp was a rich man – but some of the richest people in the galaxy had spent all their money on Trajan.

The Starchasers landed and checked into a hotel. They met up in Misha's room.

'Have we got any idea where to start looking?' asked Finn.

'Not much,' said Misha. 'But we know she's been buying stuff in this part of the planet – we've got copies of the credit bills.'

'Let's head into the shops tomorrow and start checking the place out.'

'O.K.,' said Misha. 'I'm really worried that Ella has become a shopping addict. So remember what I said guys – no shopping!'

finn goes shopping

You could buy anything on Trajan.

Rare space diamonds? They had them. Works of art from aliens that had died out a million years ago? No problem. The very latest in handbags from Earth, made of solid gold, yet light as a feather to carry? Just step this way. Anything you could possibly want, though nothing you really needed.

And if you couldn't afford it, that was no problem – you could always get credit, even if your children and grandchildren would have to pay for it.

The Starchasers wandered on and on, deeper and deeper into the planet, until at last Suma had had enough. Everywhere there were shoppers: humans and aliens from every planet in the universe, all shopping!

It was all so easy. You didn't have to carry anything. All the things you bought would be delivered, gift-wrapped, to your hotel. After all, it wasn't real money, was it? Why not just keep on spending?

'I'm getting bored to death here! We've got a job to do. Remember?'

'Sorry, Suma,' said Misha. 'I was just looking at these great designer space boots …'

'Well don't. And where's Finn?'

'Dunno. Think he may have gone in that gadget shop.'

'Oh no! Now we're in trouble.'

They went in the shop. A robot assistant was showing Finn the latest virtual world space helmet.

'Quick!' shouted Suma. 'He's about to pay for it! Grab him before it's too late!'

Finn was about to look into the machine that checked the pattern in his eye. No one had credit cards any more. They weren't safe.

But everyone's eye was different. That's how you paid for things.

Suma and Misha grabbed Finn and dragged him out of the shop. Three heavy security robots tried to stop them, but they got out just in time. Suma was really annoyed with Finn.

'What were you doing in there, you stupid Earth idiot! Did you see how much that thing cost?'

'What thing?'

'That helmet!'

'What helmet?' Finn scratched his head. 'I don't remember … Oh, yes, wait a minute, I do!'

They walked past another branch of the same gadget shop, full of customers buying expensive stuff. Suma slipped a tiny machine out of his shoulder harness and looked at the screen.

'Thought so. They're using mind probes. Putting messages into your brain to make you buy things.'

'But that's against the law!' said Misha.

'Misha, this is Trajan. Remember what Ripp Gunn said. This place is dangerous!'

misha gets a call

Just then Misha's spacephone bleeped. It was Ripp.

'Hi, Misha. Just had a report from Creditcom. Ella bought an ice-jewel necklace five minutes ago. You won't believe what it cost!'

Misha checked her Trajan shopfinder.

'That shop is only a kilometre away!
There's a flashcab over there. Get in – we
might just catch her!'

The flashcab raced down two levels, then dropped them off outside the jewellery shop. There was a dazzling display of ice diamonds in the widow. Only the richest people in the galaxy shopped here. Your credit was checked at the door. If you weren't loaded, you didn't get in.

'She'll have left by now. Any ideas?'

Misha thought. 'Maybe. Let's find the nearest food hall.'

Food was mostly free on Trajan – as long as you didn't stop shopping. The food shops checked how much you had spent before they served you. If you hadn't done enough shopping, you didn't get any food. You could get very hungry on Trajan.

All around the food hall were fast food places with food from everywhere in the galaxy. However alien you were, there was always something you would love to eat here. And it was FAST; they didn't want you to waste time eating when you could be shopping!

One of the places sold ice cream – the best in the galaxy. Misha knew Ella loved ice cream. And that's where they found her.

at the
hotel

'What do we do now?' whispered Finn. He loved ice cream too. If only they'd let him buy that helmet, he could have had some!

'We don't want to talk to her here,' said Misha. 'We need to find out where she's staying. She knows me, but she doesn't know you two. Follow her, then ring me.'

Misha disappeared. Ella finished her ice cream, then flagged down a flashcab. Suma and Finn jumped into another one.

'Follow that flashcab!'

At last Misha got a call from Suma.

'We followed her all afternoon. She spent enough money to buy a medium sized planet! How is it possible that a pair of shoes can cost more than a spaceship? Anyway, she gave up at last and headed to the Milton Hotel on level 8, sector 298. We're outside now.'

'Great work, guys. I'll be with you in ten minutes.'

The Trajan Milton Hotel had five thousand rooms, and it would take months to check them all. Luckily, not all the staff at the hotel were robots. People staying there liked real people to serve them. It was quite easy to find people to work in the big hotels. They were people that had spent all their money, and had huge debts, and couldn't afford the space fare home. They worked in the hotels until they had enough money to get home. Sometimes they died of old age first.

Finn found a hotel porter, a blue Nexian from Sirius. He showed him a picture of Ella.

'Is this person staying at the hotel?'

'I'm sorry, I'm not allowed to tell you.'

'Here's a big wodge of cash, mate.'

'She's staying in room 4379.'

Misha knocked on the door of room 4379. There was no reply, but the door wasn't locked. The Starchasers pushed their way in.

Ella was sitting at her desk. She looked up.

'Misha! What are you doing here? And who are these people? What's going on?'

Suma's whiskers were twitching. His yellow eyes were staring at Ella. His whole body was tense.

Without warning, Suma leapt on to Ella, knocking her over. His teeth were at her throat.

'Suma! What are you doing?' Misha yelled, but Suma ignored her.

'Now tell me,' he snarled. 'What have you done to Ella?'

the
clonebot

Misha and Finn leapt forward to pull Suma off Ella, but just then the bedroom door opened and in came – Ella.

She was staring at Suma in amazement.

'Misha, what are you doing here? What's going on?'

The 'Ella' that Suma had jumped on lay silent on the floor. Although Suma had bitten deeply into it, there was no blood.

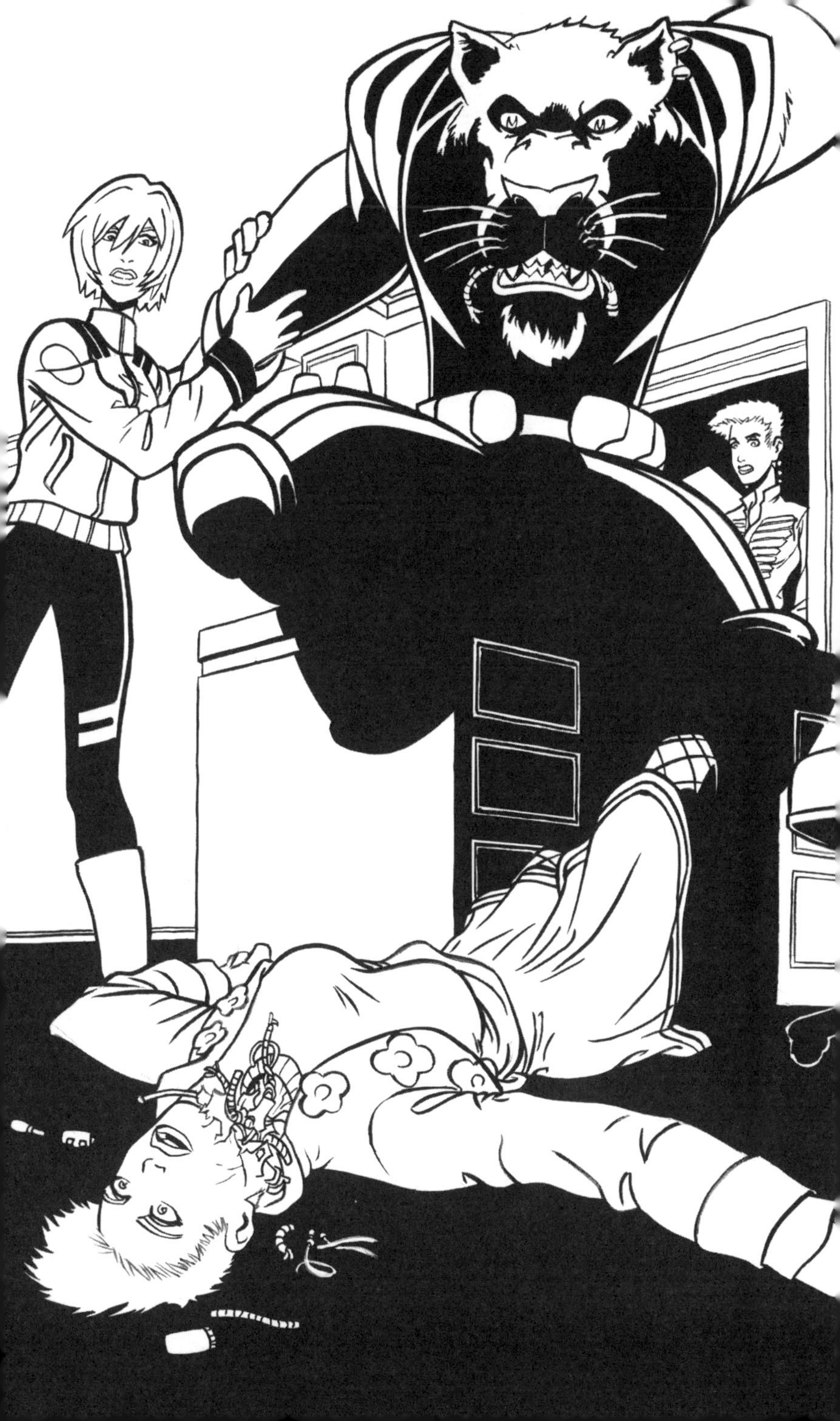

Ella saw everyone looking at it.

'It's a clonebot. It's identical to me in every way, but of course it's not human. But, whoever you are, how did you know? There's no way of telling them from real people!'

Suma's eyes flashed. This could look frightening – Misha and Finn knew it was his way of laughing. He said nothing.

'But Suma, why were you so angry?' asked Misha, changing the subject.

'How do we buy things? By looking into a machine that checks our eye patterns! The only way that this machine could do that … '

' … was if it had stolen my eyes!' laughed Ella. 'Well, as you see, my eyes are still in my head. Now, what are you doing here, and who are these guys?'

Misha went over to Ella and held her hand.

'We're the Starchasers, Ella. I've got some bad news. Your dad sent us to find you. I'm afraid – he's dying.'

Ella couldn't help herself. She sat down in the chair and started to roar with laughter.

ELLa's pLan

'Ella! Did you hear what I said? Your father is dying!'

'Is that what he told you? No he isn't, Misha. He'll live for years yet.'

'How do you know?'

'Because he's tried that one before. Look, Misha, and you Starchasers, whoever you are, sit down and listen. But promise me that you won't tell anyone else – that's for me to do.

'Making clonebots isn't allowed. If you can't tell them from real people, there are all sorts of ways you could use them for crime. But my father was determined to try. He made the first clonebot – and he made it look like me! It even had exactly the same eye pattern as I've got. Of course, it doesn't really think.'

'How does it work, then?'

'By remote control. You have to wear a virtual reality helmet. You can control everything the robot does or says. If the clonebot eats ice cream, you can even taste it!

'I knew my father was wrong to make one. I thought that if the government found out they would shut down the factory.'

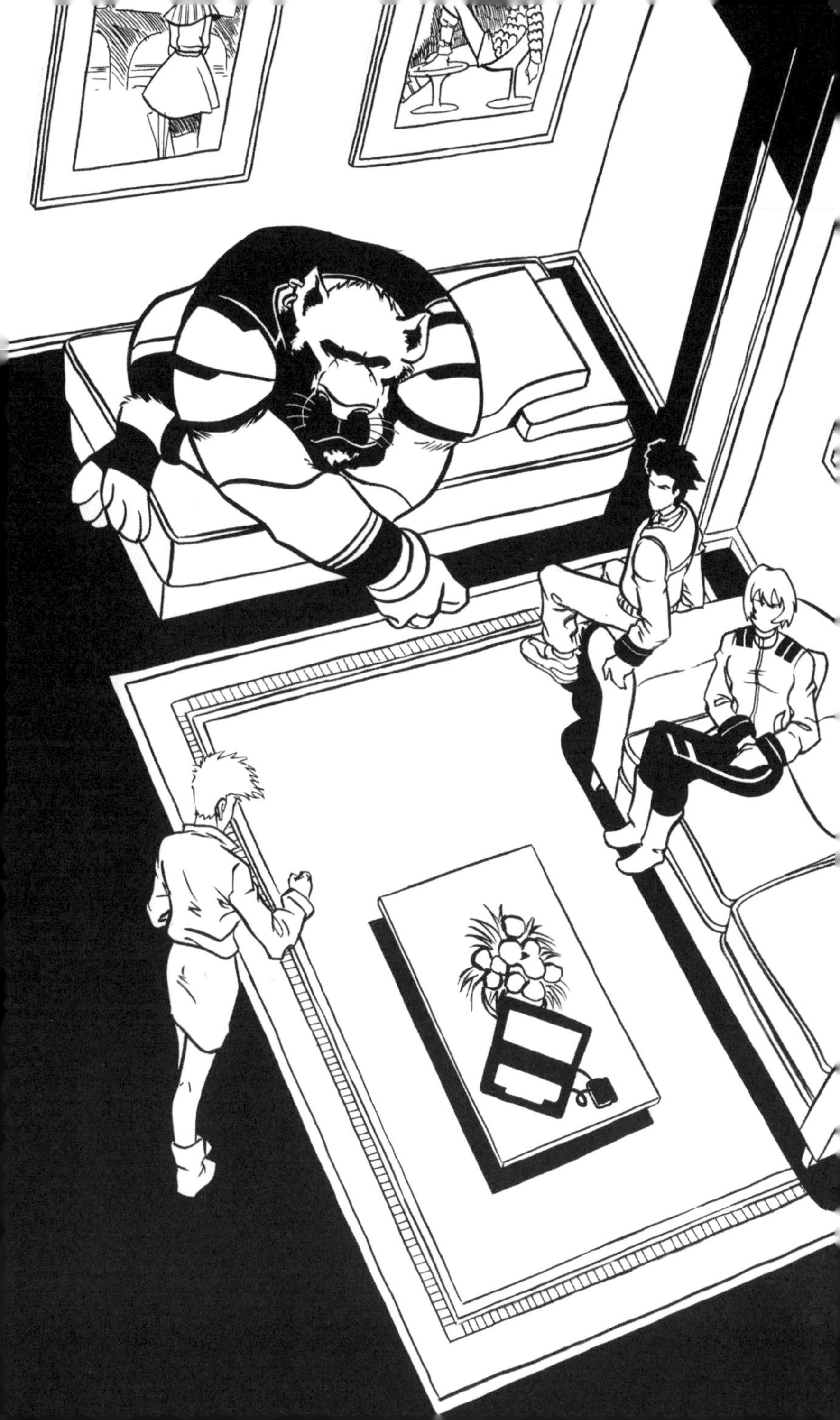

'So that was what the row was about!' said Finn.

'Yes – well, no, not exactly. Dad is really mean. He's got pots of money, but he hates me spending anything. So I came up with a plan. I pinched the clonebot and came here

to Trajan. I paid my hotel bill with cash so he couldn't track me. Then I used the robot to buy things.

'I can just imagine Dad's face when he got the bills. Of course, he can't say anything, otherwise I would go public on the clonebot!'

They all tried to imagine Ripp Gunn's face when he got the bills. It wasn't that hard, because just at that moment the door opened and Ripp Gunn came in, looking about as cheerful as someone who's just had a huge bill for something he didn't want at all.

a bit
sneaky

Ella looked shocked.

'Dad! How did you find me?'

'The Starchasers are good! I knew they would find you. I followed them to this hotel, and bribed the porter to tell me your room number.'

'That porter's having a really great day,' muttered Finn.

'Now, Ella, you are coming home with me. We've got some talking to do about these bills.'

'Talking of bills,' said Misha, 'We've done what you asked. How about paying our bill?'

'I've done it already. You can check your account if you like.'

Misha took out her spacephone and checked. The money was there, right enough.

'Thank you, Mister Gunn. Now we have the money perhaps we can talk about these illegal clonebots you have been making. I'm sure the galactic government would be very interested.'

Ripp Gunn didn't want to talk about them, but he could see he was going to have to.

'All right, but just remember this is top secret. I'm actually making them for the government!'

'Why?'

'Just think! Galaxy leaders aren't popular. Sometimes people try to kill them. It wouldn't matter if it was a clonebot! Some-

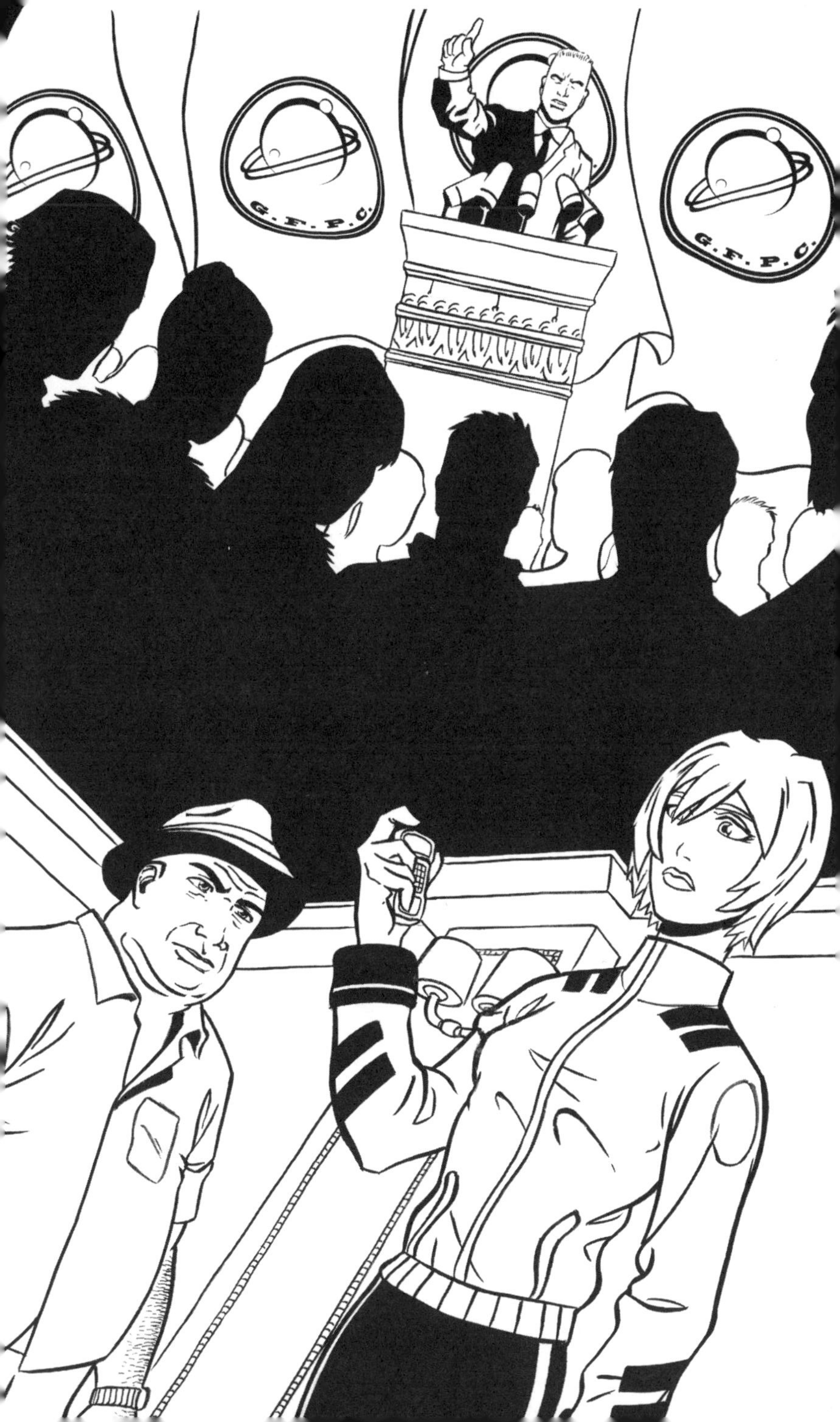
G.F.P.C.
G.F.P.C.

times they have to go to distant planets for meetings. Using a clonebot would mean they don't really have to go at all. No one would know it wasn't them!'

'Hmmm,' said Misha. 'Sounds a bit sneaky to me.'

'In any case,' said Suma. 'It won't work. I can tell humans from clonebots. And I can prove it to you.'

'Go, on prove it.'

'Easy. You're a clonebot.'

The clonebot showed Ripp Gunn's feelings really well.

'So all my work is wasted!'

'Well, maybe not,' said Suma. 'What's the deal if I can come up with a way to solve the problem?'

'Suma!' yelled Misha. 'You know that's a really bad idea!'

'Suma sighed. 'It's always the same. Every time I come up with a really good idea to make money … '

A week later, the Starchasers were back at base.

'So, Suma. How can you tell clonebots from humans? They looked pretty human to me!'

Suma just sat there, looking mysterious.

'Come on Suma, out with it!' ordered Misha.

'All right, but I'm not sure you'll want to hear this! You humans are good at lots things, but you don't have very good noses! If you did, you'd know that humans smell – a lot! – but clonebots don't smell of anything!'

LITERATURE

and

LANDSCAPE

in

East Devon

in association
with
East Devon Alliance

WRITTEN AND EDITED

by

Peter Nasmyth

Mta Publications
London

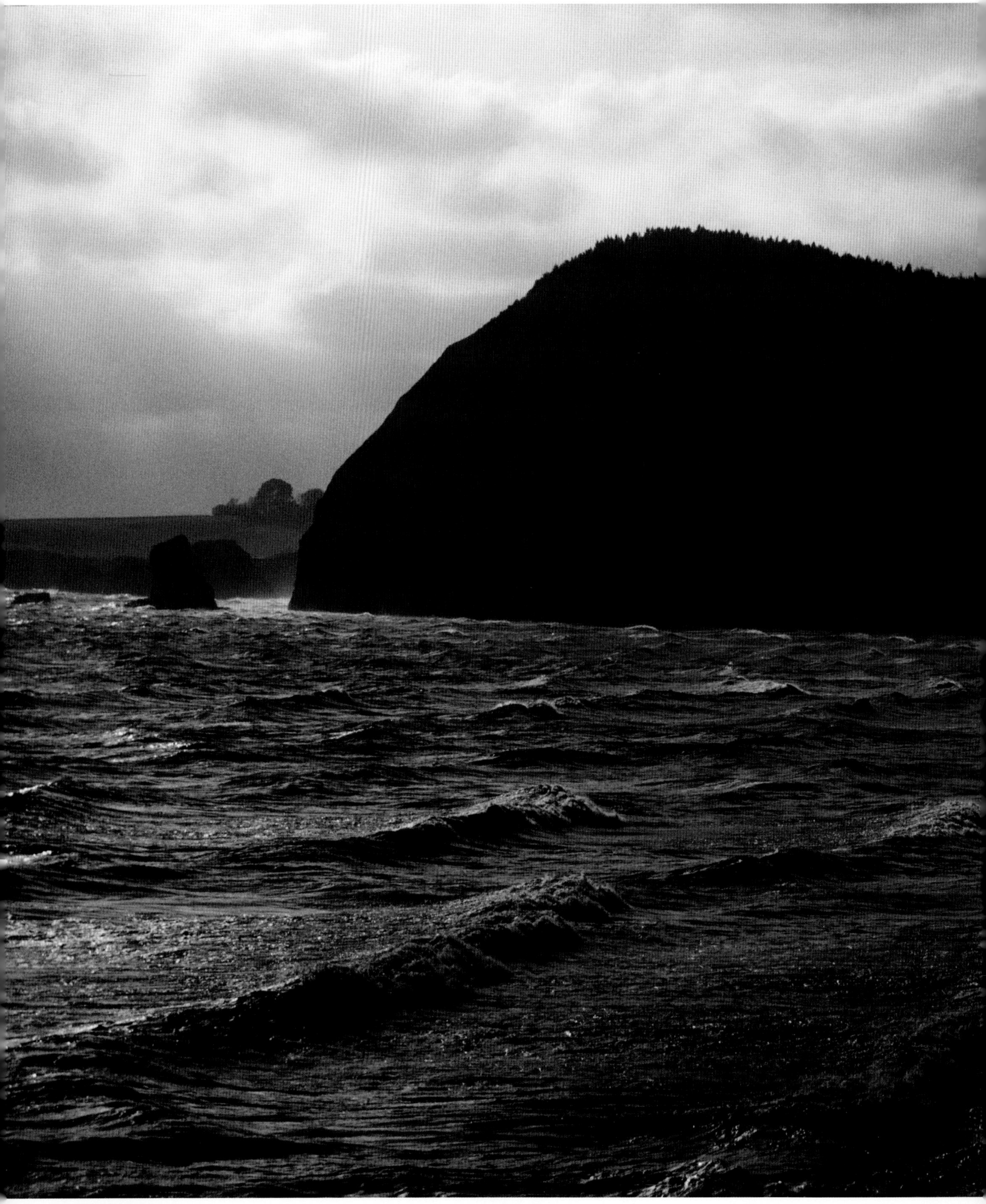

CONTENTS

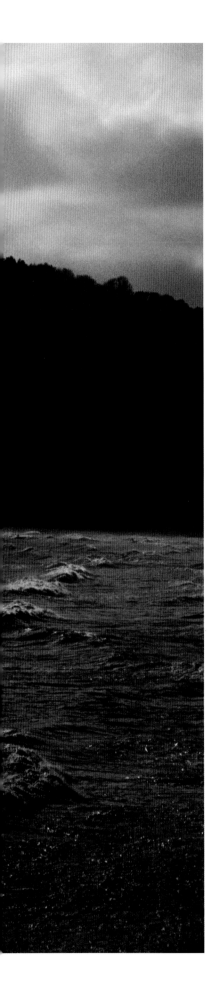

FOREWORD

PREVIOUS PAGE
Metallic sea, looking towards Ladram Bay from Jacob's Ladder at Sidmouth.

There can be few better ways of capturing the spirit inhabiting a landscape than through the literature that emerges from it. The fluid force of language moves in and around its hidden crevices like a pair of x-ray eyes born out of history. In great literature it is often said that the landscape itself can serve as a character in its own right – in that it speaks to and affects behaviour in the other dramatis personae. Thus in this book we have tried to select the most eloquent pieces of countryside and match them with localised extracts from writers who wrote within the East Devon District Council boundary. It is done with the spirit of the region's greatest literary figure, Samuel Taylor Coleridge in mind. After all it was he, along with his fellow Romantics, who saw the human mind as the crown of creation and thus the voice of nature describing itself. But to this grandiose task we have added a note of modernity, in the form of up-to-date photographs.

While some writers quoted here were born or lived in the area, others merely visited and very often changed the name-plates within their fiction. As a result, a few authors have entered this book through the back door. For instance the town of Sidmouth appears under the pseudonyms of Baymouth (**William Thackeray**); Stymouth (**Beatrix Potter**); Dynmouth (**William Trevor**); Idmouth (**Thomas Hardy**); Seacombe (**Stephen Reynolds**). Sometimes places are composites of real places. **Beatrix Potter** admits that Stymouth, although mostly Sidmouth, carries a dash of Teignmouth, Lyme Regis, and Ilfracombe. But we hope to have provided a fairly thorough overview of East Devon's main literature, even if unable, alas, to include all who wrote about the area. Our sources and areas for further research are found in the large Bibliography at the back.

In terms of style, the books and authors highlighted **in bold text** are the ones directly related to East Devon. Those left in normal script are not. The text *italicised* belongs to the writers themselves and also work titles. ***Bold and italicised*** together are the titles of the works usually under discussion.

One should also briefly mention the question that is asked implicitly throughout these pages. Given that landscape may operate as a voiceless character within so many works of fiction or poetry, what is the advice it is *truly* giving? Is it as the author envisioned – or something else? Every writer will give the messages of nature as they see them. But with no obvious defining answers, it can be a rewarding pastime to revisit the streets, pathways, fields, rivers, cliffs as described, to see if new answers are now lurking. As a result we have added descriptions of a few relevant walks for readers and the authors of the future.

View towards Wood-bury Common from the fields just above Otterton.

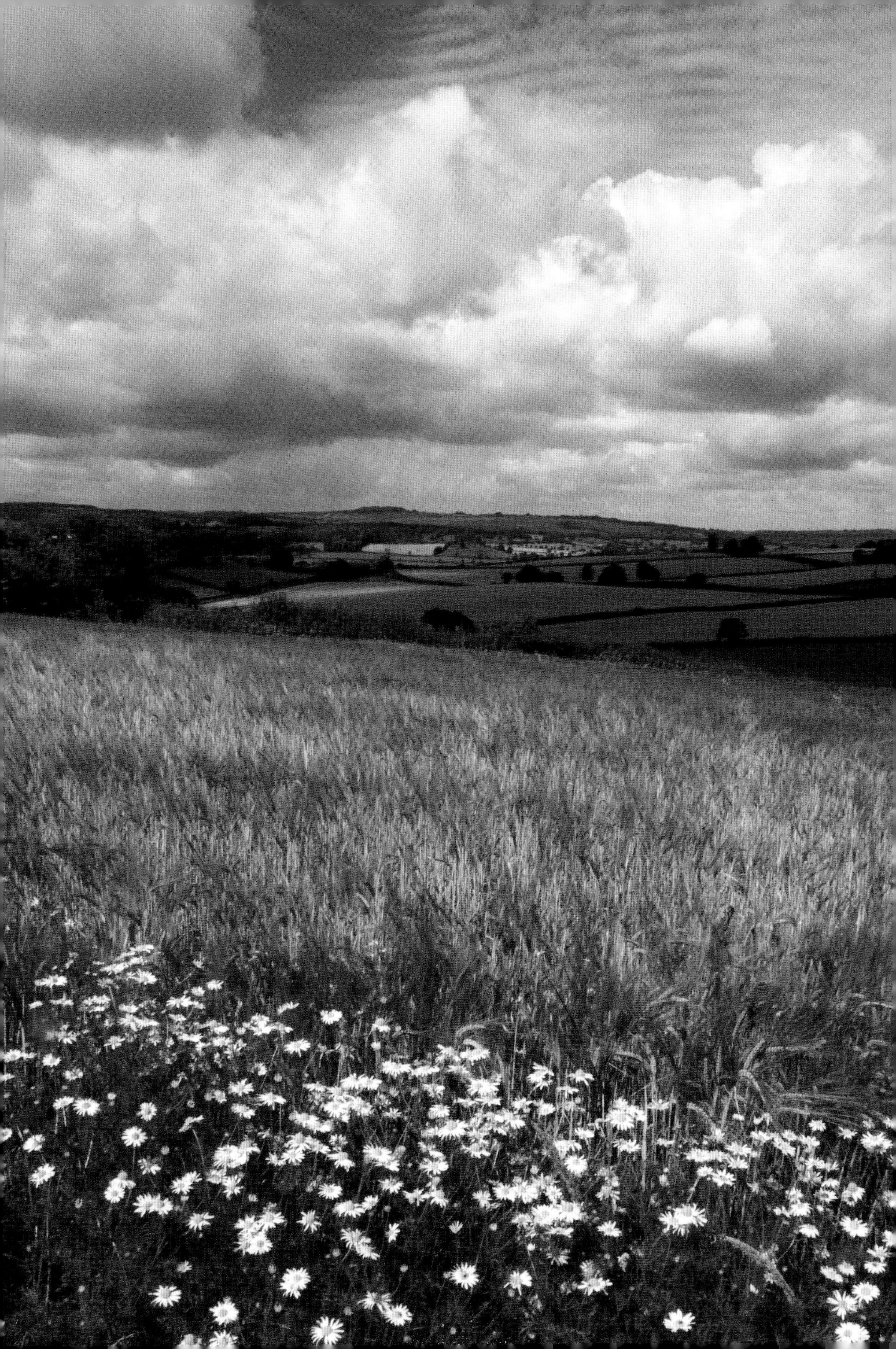

INTRODUCTION

CALL FROM A GREEN AND PLEASANT LANDSCAPE

Until the 18th century the human dwelling used to serve as the refuge from landscape, or the vastness and, as they saw it, cruelty of nature. Walk inside, shut the door, be comforted by the fire, table, stored food, family, the inventions of civilisation. But today nature is increasingly a refuge from the vastness and cruelty of the human dwelling. The need to regularly escape our swelling cities and towns into open spaces is growing exponentially. Areas free from traffic, advertisements, screens, human noise and demands, that offer the mind the calm and contemplation of open rolling hills, green fields, an undisturbed sky, are not a luxury any more. They are a psychological necessity. Hence the urgent need to judiciously preserve what is left, particularly in England, which for its size is Europe's most crowded nation.

For writers and poets, retreating to the countryside has been a regular pastime down through history, for exactly the same reasons. Linking them to landscape is not a difficult task. It is something they do readily themselves; choosing their spots carefully to encourage that grass-growing quality of the mind where thoughts can settle, concentrate and structure into a work of art. The breathing open space of the sea is a favourite. Indeed, it may not be stretching a point to claim that most great literature has grown out of the landscape; the major themes, phrases, ideas appearing miraculously as the author's eyes caressed a landscape, or were themselves caressed by one.

This book is about writers who sought such inspiration in one unique section of the English countryside – East Devon, and the places they found that gave it back in abundance. It is also a call for the preservation of these places and the vital experience they bestow. Writers and artists often lead the general population in behaviour trends. Today, with increasing levels of free-time, more and more people than ever aspire to become writers and artists themselves, which can only be a good thing. It also means that the tranquillity and calm found in peaceful but accessible areas of countryside, is turning into a bankable resource.

Looking out across East Devon's undulating green hills and open fields that lead to a sparkling expanse of sea, is a feeling in itself and one loved universally. Famously beautiful areas like East Devon offer these sights and spaces in generous quantities, and have been recognised as such by previous generations. The administrative district contains two Areas of Outstanding Natural Beauty (AONB), making it proportionately among the UK's largest AONBs. Virtually all of its seaboard is a World Heritage Site, the Jurassic Coast. The landscape is imbued with the perfect antidote to our increasing population density. But this very quality is now threatened, as East Devon's demographic increases beyond the region's capacity to usefully contain it. While this threat extends across the entire country as world population multiplies alarmingly, it stands as the duty of those who inhabit a landscape to give it a voice.

But importantly, this book is not a NIMBY (Not In My Backyard) loudhailer, because places like this are equally important for the growing number of us without backyards. In East Devon statistics confirming this were discovered by accident during the 'Save our Sidmouth' campaign against the District Council's plan to develop the town's elegant park, The Knowle. Part of the campaign involved manning a display in the town centre - aimed at raising awareness in the East Devon District Council catchment. To the campaigners' surprise, of the 4209 objecting names and addresses against the Council's planning application (to itself), approximately 75% were from non-locals, mostly holiday-makers and visitors from other parts of Devon and the UK.

This implies that every landscape carries its own optimum level of population; a number beyond which more inhabitants no longer enhance the local economy and lifestyle, but quietly sabotage it. The fields, streets, hills, footpaths, shorelines of East Devon now carry more than enough human occupants to provide the evolving requirements of enterprise. The local economy is increasingly leisure, and the population increasingly older, thus adjusting the region's definition of leisure.

Writers and photographers understand this better than most. The majority of the authors quoted in this book have been active campaigners in preserving our historic landscape. **Beatrix Potter** personally saved significant areas of the Lake District; **John Fowles**, as curator of the Lyme Regis Museum loudly promoted local conservation; **Eden Phillpotts** served as a dedicated President of the Dartmoor Preservation Association; **John Betjeman** created the Victorian Society and saved London's magnificent St Pancras Hotel from the 1960s developers (and many other fine buildings). Even **Jane Austen**, in her portrait of *Sanditon* (often believed to be Sidmouth) in her unfinished novel, did her bit in discreetly satirising purely finance-driven development.

Every photograph in these pages is haunted by the presence of those who lived in or tended that particular vista or building before us. As locals, the least we can do is remind the custodians of the countryside and those handing out planning permissions of the huge responsibility they exercise, not only historically, but now for human health. The voice of the landscape desperately needs to be heard. This book tries in a very small way, to cup some hands around its mouth.

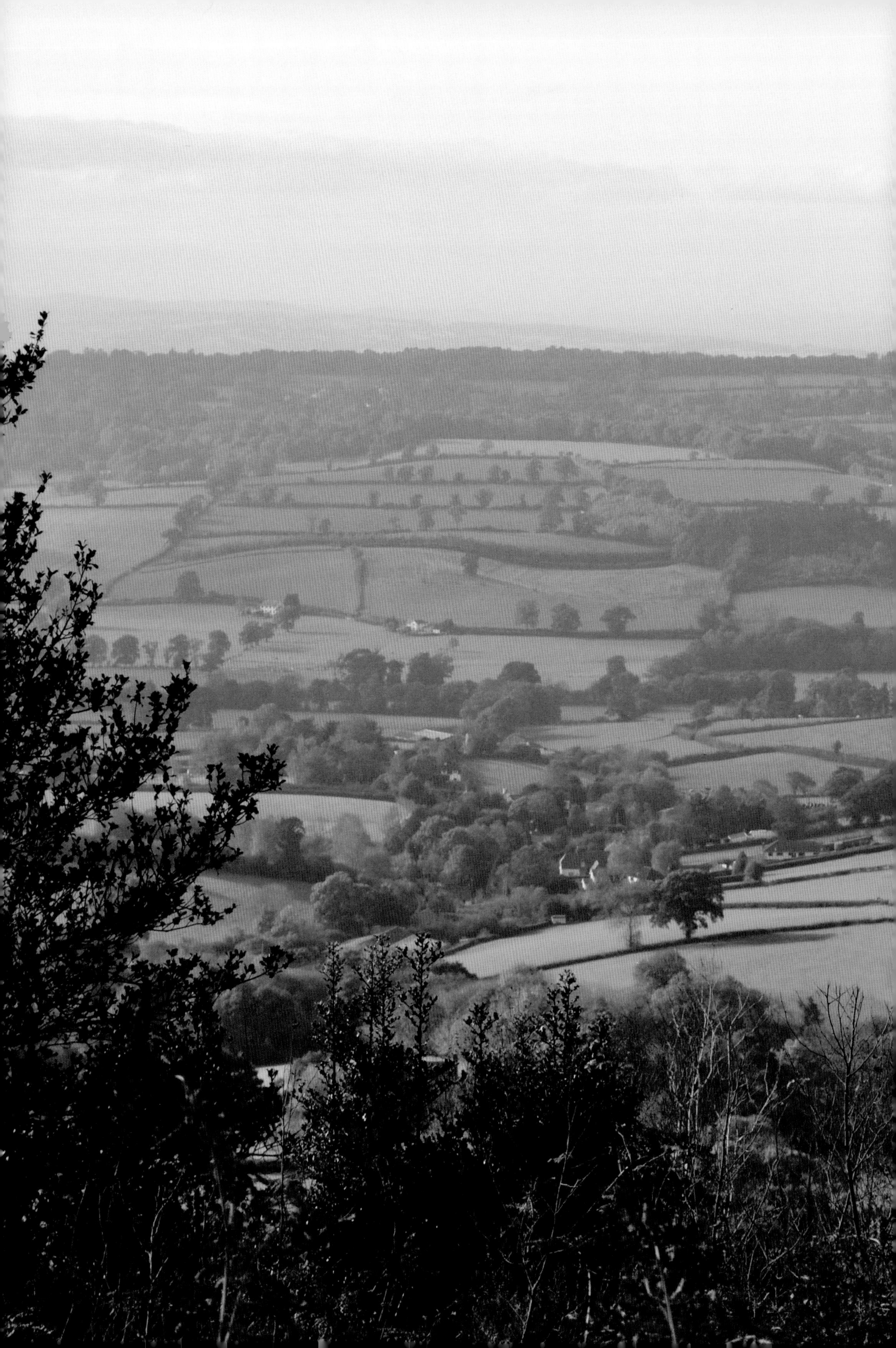

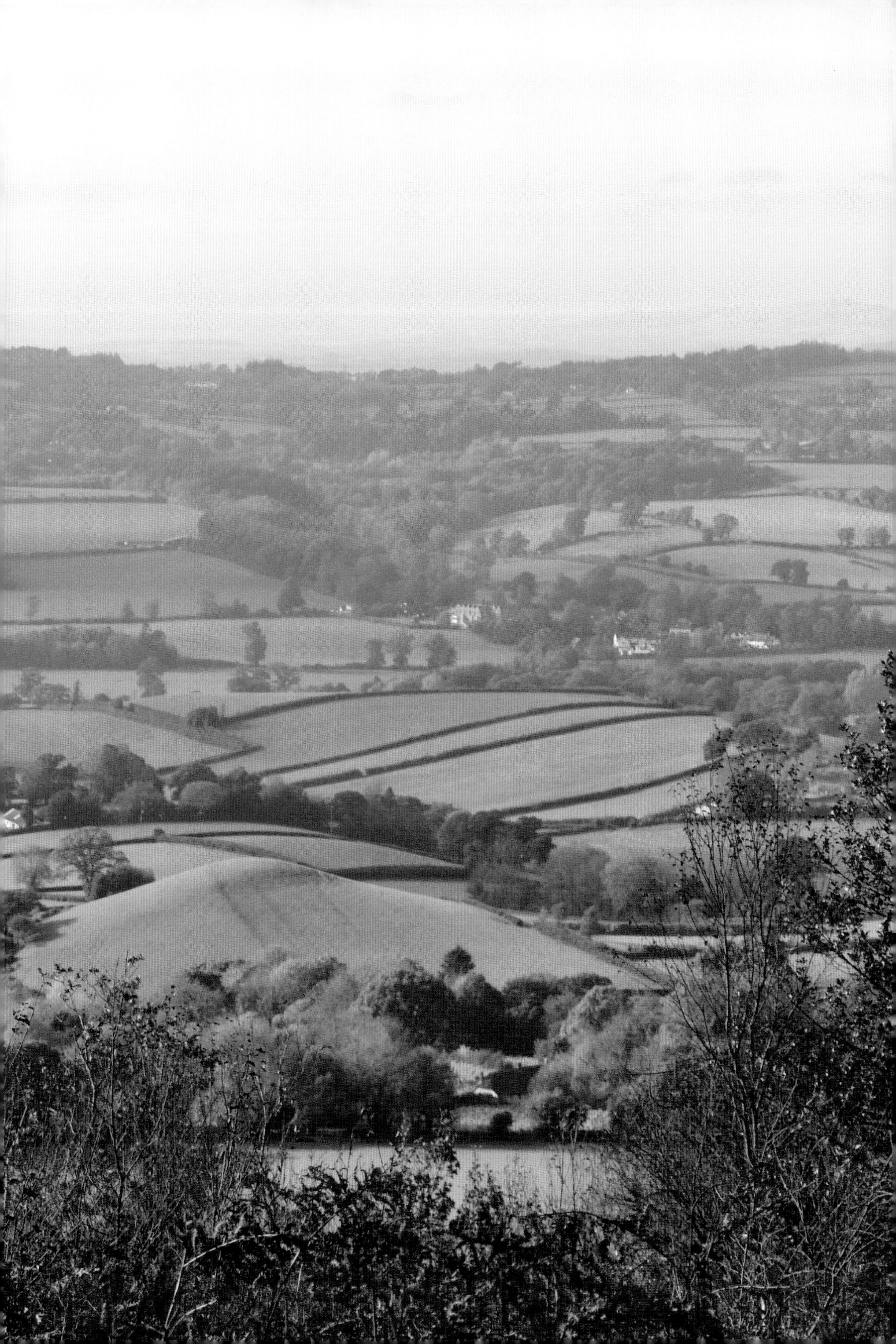

PREVIOUS PAGE
Looking down on the Otter valley from East Hill. Some claim this area is that of 'The Burrows' in the Harry Potter books (see page 98).

Samuel Taylor Coleridge, by an unknown German artist; at around the age he wrote *Songs of the Pixies.*

1 OTTERY ST MARY 'My sweet birthplace'

'I love fields and woods and mountains with almost a visionary fondness… and because I have found benevolence and quietness growing within me as that fondness has increased, therefore I should wish to be the means of implanting it in others.'
Samuel Taylor Coleridge in a 1799 letter to his brother George.

These words of the poet **Samuel Taylor Coleridge** (1772-1834) are a perfect launch-pad for this journey into the lush and welcoming landscape of East Devon. Written by the region's greatest man of letters, they emanate from its centre with a strong clue as to how the woods and fields of his native Devon started a process that, with his friend **William Wordsworth,** changed the tenor of British poetry for ever. These two inaugural Romantic Poets would promote a new creed idealising landscape and the intelligence of nature within it, setting up human imagination and individuality as its cutting edge. With these new philosophical beliefs held aloft they would shake the tiring world of the Enlightenment so powerfully, the effects are still keenly felt today.

To see how this was started, let us join the young Samuel Coleridge on the banks of his beloved river Otter, as the 19th century loomed on the horizon. This bright pair of Devonshire eyes absorbed the Otter valley and little else for his first nine years of life. Growing up in the nearby market town of Ottery St Mary, itself grown up around one of the crossings for East Devon's most central river the Otter, this youngest of ten, much doted-on son of the headmaster of the local King's School (and also vicar of Ottery) discovered his freedom from classes, parents and bullying elder brothers in books. He read them as often as possible, on the Otter's red sandstone banks. Flanked on either side by undulating woodlands and fields rising up on its East and West Hills, the child's vivid animistic mind would have probed the leafy shadows and shimmering depths of water, primed with imagery he absorbed from his father's library.

The young Sam was a precocious reader. He read the entire *'Arabian Nights'* at the age of six and was so affected by dreams and nightmares that his father had to burn his copy. We know the river played a crucial role in his early life due to the poems and references he made to it later. Indeed one of his early poems, written at the age of 21, is his **Sonnet: To the River Otter** (1793) in which he addresses the river as a personal friend, beginning with the words, *'Dear native brook!'*

…so deep imprest
Sink the sweets scenes of childhood, that mine eyes
I never shut amid the sunny ray,
But straight with all their tints thy waters rise,
Thy crossing plank, thy marge with willows grey
And bedded sand that vein'd with various dyes
Gleamed through thy bright transparence!

Here one catches glimpses of the bright transparence of language that would investigate human emotion with such originality. Five years later it generated one of the most discussed poems in the English language, **Kubla Khan** (1798). Furthermore his East Devon riverbank would also cut a profound psychological mark into his character when at the age of seven he was caught by his mother brandishing a kitchen knife at his bullying brother Frank. Fearing a beating he ran away from the house and hid where no one could find him – in one of his haunts beside the Otter. He sat there in a state of raging fear reading devoutly from a prayer book and thinking *'with inward and gloomy satisfaction how miserable my mother must be.'*

The result was he ended up spending the night out and nearly dying, having fallen asleep and rolled down to within a few feet of the water. Luckily he was found at daybreak and carried home frozen and semi-conscious, to be greeted by his parents who were *'outrageous with joy.'*

As a child alone out in the woods and fields for a night, he would have experienced the raw forces of nature deeply imprinted into his mind: the kind which, with the aid of opium, may well have expanded into the lines

'Sacred' to the child, the River Otter and Cadhay bridge, near where the young Sam was rescued.

Through wood and dale the sacred river ran,
Then reached the caverns measureless to man,

as later depicted in **Kubla Khan.** The power of the child's *Arabian Nights'* fuelled imagination would certainly have filled the darkening river, woods and trees with a mix of the wild characters and creatures which inhabited the local myths and folk tales of Devon, quite possibly with *'flashing eyes'* and *'floating hair.'*

Such stories would have been fed to him in books, by his parents and friends, and on the King's School playground; stories themselves growing directly out of the landscape. Goblins, pixies and fairies would have hopped around inside those shadows. Fairies – as a mischievous, magical and tiny people, always appeal strongly to children, then as now – witness the popularity of Harry Potter's wizardry lessons. There seems a curious inevitability in the fact that Harry Potter himself also seems to carry a strong link to the Otter valley – see page 98.

But these East Devon pixies (or 'pysgies' they say in strongest Devonian) and fairies, as the semi-human mouthpieces of the landscape, also seeped out of the earth and into the body of English Romantic literature. Coleridge wrote another poem dedicated to them around the same time, **Songs of the Pixies** (1793), on one of his many return visits to his family home. Again it is set on the same river bank. Below are extracts from the text, including his full introduction,

COLERIDGE

presenting the local landmark of Pixies' Parlour. This is a place also well familiar to any child growing up in today's Ottery St Mary. The poem paints a lively portrait of a pixie (as Coleridge) welcoming a group of ladies to their secret cell beside the river Otter, then crowning one as Queen. One can already feel in this text, presentiments of his future as a revolutionary poet and philosopher in references to himself as the *'youthful Bard, unknown to Fame,'* who'd come to woo *'the Queen of Solemn Thought'.*

SONGS OF THE PIXIES

The Pixies, in the superstition of Devonshire, are a race of beings invisibly small, and harmless or friendly to man. At a small distance from a village in that county, half-way up a wood-covered hill, is an excavation called the Pixies' Parlour. The roots of old trees form its ceiling; and on its sides are innumerable cyphers, among which the author discovered his own cypher and those of his brothers, cut by the hand of their childhood. At the foot of the hill flows the river Otter. To this place the Author, during the summer months of the year 1793, conducted a party of young ladies; one of whom, of stature elegantly small, and of complexion colourless yet clear, was proclaimed the Faery Queen. On which occasion the following Irregular Ode was written.

…Thither, while the murmuring throng
Of wild-bees hum their drowsy song,
By Indolence and Fancy brought,
A youthful Bard, 'unknown to Fame,'
Woos the Queen of Solemn Thought…

Pixies' Parlour. Out of this Otter sandstone cave the pixies emerged into the Devon landscape. It is much smaller than in Coleridge's day, and further away from the river, high up on the cliffside.

COLERIDGE

…Where wearied with his flower-caressing sport,
Supine he slumbers on a violet bank;
Then with quaint music hymn the parting gleam
By lonely Otter's sleep-persuading stream;
Or where his wave with loud unquiet song
Dash'd o'er the rocky channel froths along;
Or where, his silver waters smooth'd to rest,
The tall tree's shadow sleeps upon his breast…

…Welcome, Ladies! to the cell
Where the blameless Pixies dwell:
But thou, Sweet Nymph! proclaim'd our Faery Queen…

Walking among the fields and hills around present-day Ottery St Mary one can easily pick up the scent of the late 18th-century village inhabited by the young Coleridge. Pixies' Parlour is still in evidence set in a cliff overlooking the Otter about a mile south of the town, although the course of the river has since changed. Furthermore the town developed a Pixie Day tradition, clearly fostered by Coleridge's poem. According to legend, on the Saturday closest to June 21st every year (the summer solstice), the pixies run from their cave and invade Ottery to kidnap the bell-ringers (apparently pixies are intensely annoyed by church bells). They then 'pixie lead' them back to their dell by the river. Ottery's children perform a version of this suitably adorned – although the journey has been shortened to the town square and the bell-ringers seem delighted to be kidnapped. However the dastardly power of the pixies is overcome when one of the bell ringers declares 'God rest my soul and St Mary's,' at which point they are promptly un-mazed (the pixie trance is broken) and restored to their rightful place in the church.

The Devonshire landscape spawned not only pixies and fairies in human imagination but also a corresponding architecture on the ground. This too would act powerfully on the future poet, especially within that moody, self-indulgent childhood he described to his friend Thomas Poole in 1797 as *'My Father was very fond of me and I was my mother's darling; in consequence I was very miserable.'*

Indeed, although he was sent away from Ottery at the age of nine after the death of his father, he remained proud of his birthplace and maintained his Devon accent all his life.

The physical place of his birth stood right in the centre of Ottery St Mary, at the School House beside the Rectory, which is no longer in existence. Directly opposite stood the town's grand 14th-century church described by the historian W.G. Hoskins as *'perhaps the finest church in Devon other than Exeter cathedral.'* Its large and prominent graveyard effectively became the young Sam's front garden where he would *'run up and down the church-yard and act over all I had been reading on the docks, the nettles and the rank-grass.'*

Standing beneath its superb crenellated towers, studded with gargoyles, it is possible to imagine the child poet staring up, unconsciously turning them into mastheads for what in his later philosophy he would call the *'New Sensibility of Feeling.'* Without doubt this magnificent building etched itself deeply into memory. Indeed the sound of its bells re-appears in his poem **Frost at Midnight** (1798):

...With unclosed lids already had I dreamt
Of my sweet birth-place, and the old church-tower
Whose bells, the poor man's only music, rang
From morn to evening, all the hot Fair-day,
So sweetly, that they stirred and haunted me
With a wild pleasure, falling on mine ear
Most like articulate sounds of things to come!

The graveyard of Ottery church with Chanter's House in the background, home of the Coleridge family from the poet's day until 2006.

It could be that the church bells rang like a summons to the prophetic ear. Those *'things to come'* would include **The Rime of the Ancient Mariner** (1797). The poem inspired many editions and draws on that other primary element of East Devon ever-present in the young Coleridge's imagination, the sea.

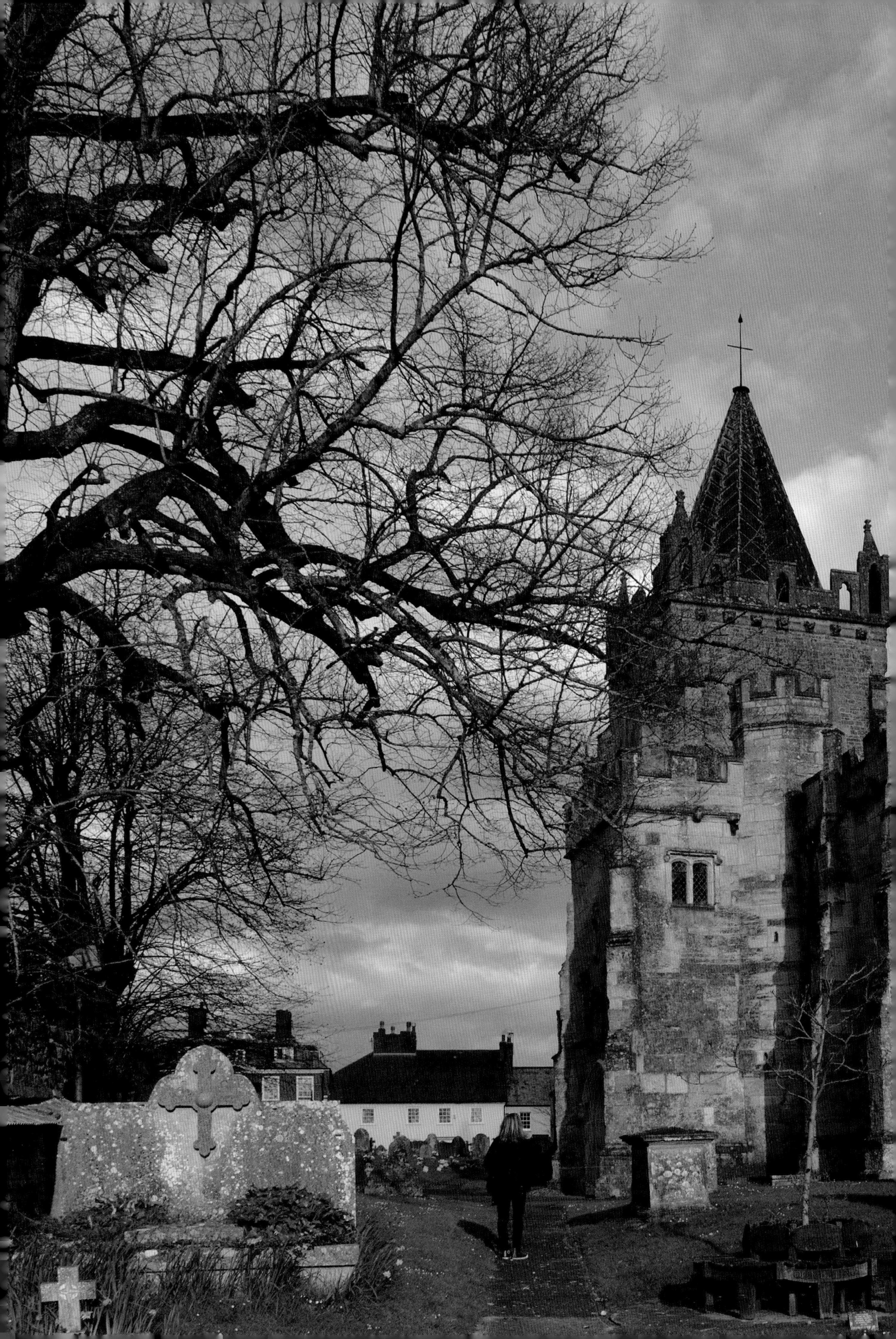

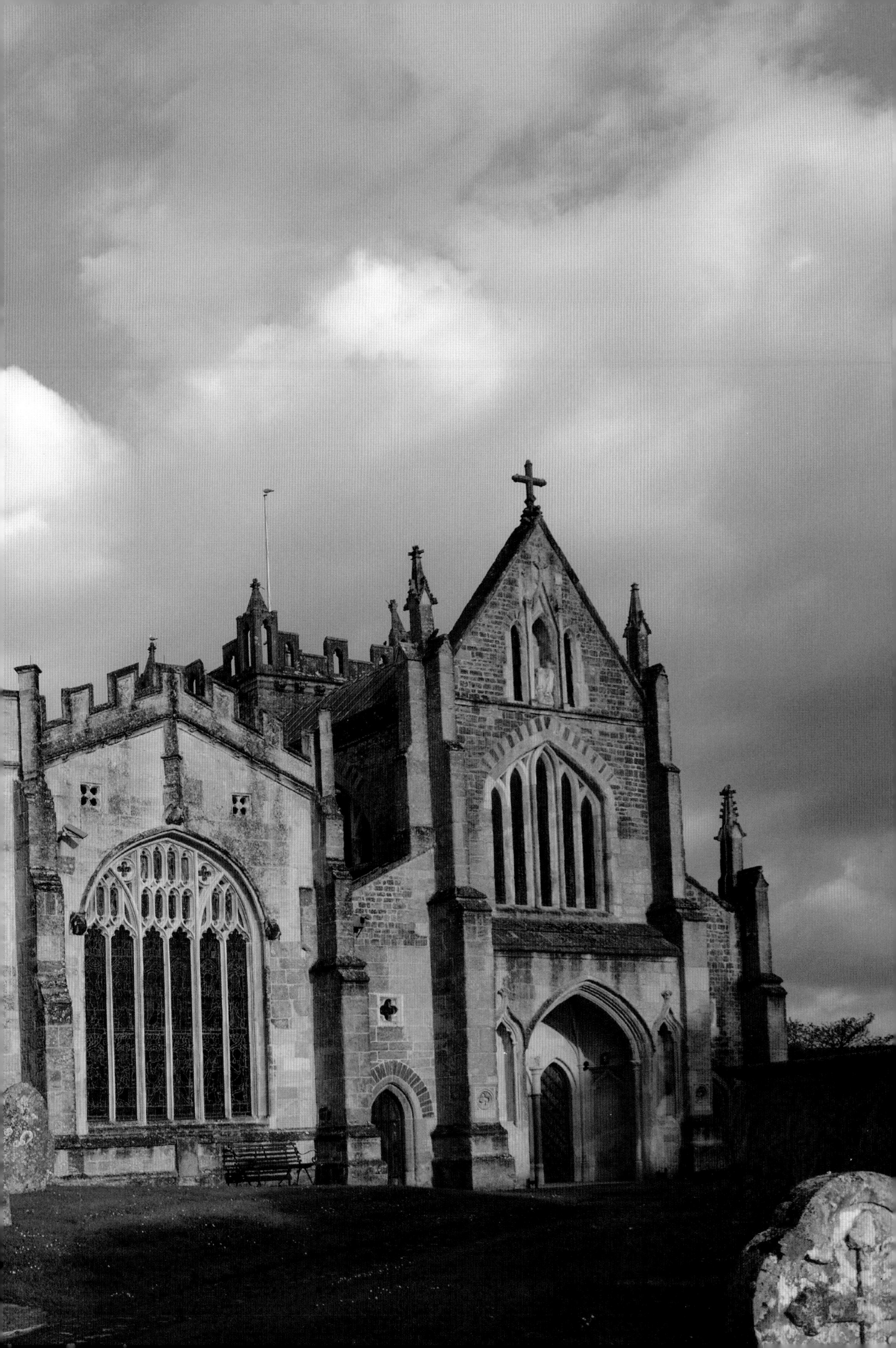

I Know the Man that Must Hear Me, by Gustav Doré. One of his illustrations of *The Rime of the Ancient Mariner*, the kind of mental image of the sea, quite possibly held by the young Coleridge growing up in nearby Ottery.

In tandem with his poetry he wrote numerous essays on contemporary philosophy and literature. These works laid out the Romantic road for those who followed – Byron, Shelley, Keats, and thence their followers further a-field, such as Pushkin and Lermontov in Russia, where poetry evolved into revolution on the streets. In his idealisation of the perceptions of childhood, this son of the river Otter saw his Devon landscape as belonging to the purified kingdom of the imagination. This is the place where the child's eye roved brilliant, free, 'filled with Nature,' before its inevitable 'exile' into the adult world. The Romantics regarded humankind as the offspring of Nature, and therefore effectively its mouthpiece. Descriptions of landscape by any great poet could thus be presented as the landscape describing itself. They believed that the poetic imagination was born within the raging perceptions of childhood, a philosophical stance promoted by **William Wordsworth's** 1804 poem ***Intimations of Immortality from Recollections of Early Childhood.*** The period when, *'The earth, and every common sight To me did seem Apparell'd in celestial light The glory and the freshness of a dream...'*

WORDSWORTH

18

Ultimately East Devon would also summon this other great English poet for a visit. Not long before he became Poet Laureate, Wordsworth was spotted standing quietly inside Ottery church, clearly in an act of homage to the extraordinary friendship he'd achieved with the, by then, several-years-dead Coleridge. Indeed the spirit of the Coleridge family would remain in Ottery St Mary right up to the present. Samuel's brother James purchased the town's largest mansion, the 18 bedroom Chanter's House next to the church. The family of Lord and Lady Coleridge remained there in continuous residence until 2006 when finally it was put up for sale. Around this time the house's orchard was sold off to accommodate Ottery St Mary's new Sainsburys.

PREVIOUS PAGE
St Mary's church at Ottery. Consecrated in 1260 and rebuilt in 1335 by John Grandisson the Bishop of Exeter. Coleridge was born directly opposite at the School House, which no longer exists.

Walk 1 - S.T. Coleridge. To Pixies Parlour

For those wishing to follow in the footsteps of the poet, or pixies, there is a Coleridge Link trail running along the eastern side of the river Otter starting from below the road bridge near the old factory. It follows the river downstream, eventually crossing a small bridge into open fields. The path then climbs and dives into the wooded cliff area. Shortly afterwards the Parlour is encountered on the left as a small cave in the Otter sandstone (for photo see page 13). It is currently unmarked and much smaller than in Coleridge's day. The total distance of about half a mile is short by Coleridge's standards. He thought nothing of walking the ten miles to Ottery from the Cullompton coach-stop. But it is still possible to pick up the poet's spirit and 'walk in gladness' to the Parlour and beyond.

The Ship Fled the Storm, by the French artist Gustav Doré (1832-83). Illustration from *The Rime of the Ancient Mariner.*

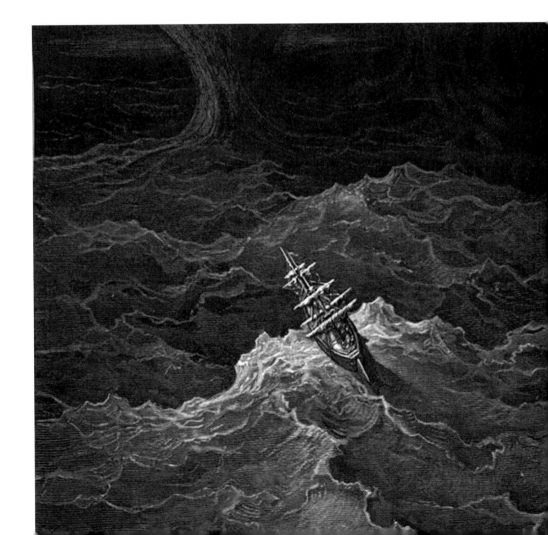

View towards Feniton and Larkbeare from just above Honiton. Otter valley in the foreground.

THACKERAY

2 LARKBEARE

The inland farms and fields of East Devon are the region's heartland. As agriculture developed over the centuries the surface of the land was cleared, enclosed, hedged, cropped, cattled and sheeped. Population centres slowly grew up around the river bridges and market towns, fed by the increasingly prosperous farmland. But the overall geological features changed very little. The Axe and Otter rivers switched course but only within their flood-plain boundaries. With the industrial revolution in the 19th century, Devon's population declined as the factories outside the region offered higher wages. But this demographic trend has now dramatically reversed. Today the landscape has been going through an unprecedented upheaval. With the internet and home-working many people are now fleeing the cities out into the calmer countryside. New-build housing has been leaping across the farmland not just in ones and twos, but blocks of 100 plus. Three years ago a whole new town, Cranbrook 'landed' onto East Devon's Development Plan, with a promise of 8,000 new homes. 1,000 are already built.

Three miles from the centre of Cranbrook and half a mile from the new A30 lies the sleepy hamlet of Larkbeare, the place where the writer **William Makepeace Thackeray** (1811-63) lived for five years from 1824, when not away boarding at Charterhouse. It was in and around these mid-Devon farmlands that he set the opening chapters of his novel *Pendennis* (1849) which appeared shortly after his greatest work *Vanity Fair* (1848). In the novel the young Arthur Pendennis, whose age and circumstances bear a remarkable similarity to the teenage Thackeray's, finds himself established in the nearby stately home of Fairoaks, again uncannily similar to today's Escot House. Nearby Larkbeare House, where Thackeray stayed, was then in the Escot estate, home of the Kennaway family. It is said that the character Major Pendennis is a disguised portrait of Sir John Kennaway. The fictional town of Clavering St Mary lay 'nearly a mile' away with its 'old abbey church.' This is hard to distinguish from the real Ottery St Mary, itself just over a mile almost due south of Escot. He describes the church's 'great grey towers, of which the sun illuminates the delicate carving, deepening the shadows of the great buttresses and gilding the glittering windows and flaming vanes.'

But the similarities are not merely geographical. The novel opens with a great declaration of love from the then eighteen-year old Arthur Pendennis for an actress he intends to marry - to the horror of all his family. It is said that

THACKERAY

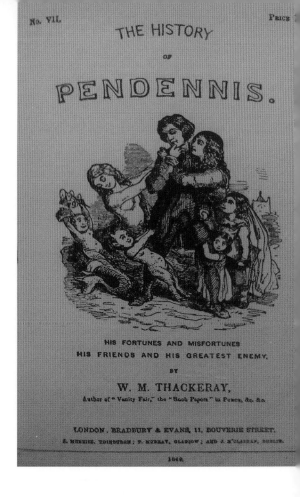

Thackeray himself while at Larkbeare also fell for an actress playing at an Exeter theatre. One can sense a certain amusement in Thackeray's re-creation of the event, and probably embellishment of the facts from the safety of some 20 years. The novel also mentions the moment this aspiring young Byron achieved his first-ever publication *'in the Poets' Corner of the County Chronicle, with some verses with which he was perfectly well satisfied.'* Later the publication's full title is spelled out as *The County Chronicle and Chatteris Champion*.

Again real life comes up with a strong parallel. Chatteris is Thackeray's code name for Exeter and a similarly-aged **William Thackeray** received his first publication in Exeter's *Western Luminary* in 1828. However the work is not a love poem but a satire called **Irish Melody,** parodying a speech by the Irish politician Lalor Sheil.

Reading **Pendennis** in 21st-century East Devon is more interesting for the details of early 19th-century daily life, particularly its first 50 pages (the rest are a poor match to **Vanity Fair**). For instance he describes the young Pen riding into Chatteris (Exeter) where he meets a friend who has just ridden from Baymouth (Sidmouth), who exclaims: *"Just look at my leader--did you ever see a prettier animal? Drove over from Baymouth. Came the nine mile in two-and-forty minutes. Not bad going, sir."*

Not bad indeed. Forty two minutes from Sidmouth to the centre of Exeter by horse... this is faster than today's 52A bus. The fact receives further explanation when the friend invites Arthur Pendennis to join him at a play that evening. Pen decides to accept because he calculates he can make the return eight miles ride home to Clavering St Mary afterwards because *'there was a moonlight.'* The image of the young Thackeray riding across East Devon at midnight in 1828, possibly cantering down the Rockbeare Straight, is as vivid as anything in the plot.

But it is not geographical description for which Thackeray is known, rather his delightful light-touch irony, as in his description of Pen's mother: *'I think it is not national prejudice which makes me believe that a high-bred English lady is the most complete of all Heaven's subjects in this world.'* Also for the statement on the book's cover (see photo) which titles the novel as **The History of Pendennis, his Fortunes and Misfortunes, his Friends and his Greatest Enemy** (the latter is surely himself).

While most agree that **Vanity Fair** is the superior book, anyone coming to **Pendennis** today might use the following crib sheet on his East Devon synonyms:

Clavering St Mary = Ottery St Mary
Chatteris = Exeter
Baymouth = Sidmouth
The River Brawl = the River Otter
Fairoaks = Escot House

Walk 2 - William Thackeray. Escot to Ottery

Escot Park is open to the public, with many fine views of Fairoaks (Escot). A pleasant walk can be taken down from the house to the River Tale then downstream more or less following its course until it joins the River Brawl (the Otter). Turn downstream again and continue Pen's walk to Clavering St Mary (Ottery). It involves a short section of minor road over Cadhay Bridge (see photo page 12). The total distance is just under two miles each way.

Escot House, renamed Fairoaks by Thackeray, home of the Kennaway family who sometimes hosted the young William. They still occupy it today.

3 ROCKBEARE to Honiton

Just to the west of Larkbeare lies the old Roman road the Fosse Way, today known as the Rockbeare Straight. This used to be the main artery into the county from London. Now virtually empty, (replaced by the new A30 just to the south), it has conveyed many an important traveller westward, including the creator of Sherlock Holmes, **Arthur Conan Doyle** (1859-1930) who visited Devon many times. He worked as a doctor for a short period in 1882 near Plymouth. For further details of his visits to the area, that include his career in cricket, see page 96.

Doyle's meticulous, neo-gothic imagination found itself drawn further on down the road, to the swirling mists and bogs of the moors which he loved. *The Hound of the Baskervilles* is set on Dartmoor. Meanwhile his more sober literary self, which he rated higher (hence his repeated attempts to kill off Holmes) devoted itself to depicting the real events of history. It is less known that he wrote a number of excellent historical novels, the first of which is set mainly in the West Country. *Micah Clarke* (1889) tells the epic story of the Monmouth Rebellion of 1685. The Duke of Monmouth had landed with twenty men at what is now Monmouth Bay, on East Devon's boundary with Lyme Regis. His mission was simple – to claim the crown of England from King James. But first he needed an army.

The story of its creation is told through the eyes of his central character, Micah Clarke, one of the rebels who watches the Duke gather an extraordinary fighting force out of the landscape by the power of oratory and reputation alone. The passage below vividly describes the assembly of troops in the East Devon area.

Extract From *Micah Clarke*

The first foot regiment, if so rudely formed a band could be so called, consisted of men of the sea, fishers and coast-men, clad in the heavy blue jerkins and rude garb of their class. They were bronzed, weather-beaten tarpaulins, with hard mahogany faces, variously armed with birding pieces, cutlasses or pistols. I have a notion that it was not the first time that those weapons had been turned against King James's servants, for the Somerset and Devon coasts were famous breeding-places for smugglers, and many a saucy lugger was doubtless lying up the creek or in bay whilst her crew had gone a-soldiering to Taunton.

As to discipline, they had no notion of it, but rolled along in true blue-water style, with many a shout and halloo to each other or to the crowd. From Star Point to Portland Roads there would be few nets for many weeks to come and fish would swim the narrow seas which should have been heaped on Lyme Cobb or exposed for sale in Plymouth market. Each group, or band, of these

CONAN DOYLE

men of the sea bore with it its own banner, that of Lyme in the front, followed by Topsham, Colyford, Bridport, Sidmouth, Otterton, Abbotsbury, and Charmouth, all southern towns, which are on or near the coast. So they trooped past us, rough and careless, with caps cocked, and the reek of their tobacco rising up from them like the steam of a tired horse. In number they must have been four hundred or thereabouts.

CONAN DOYLE

   The peasants of Rockbeare, with flail and scythe, led the next column, followed by the banner of Honiton, which was supported by two hundred stout lacemakers from the banks of the Otter. These men showed by the colour of their faces that their work kept them within four walls, yet they excelled their peasant companions in their alert and soldierly bearing. Indeed with all the troops we observed that though the countrymen were the stouter and the heartier, the craftsmen were the most ready to catch the air and spirit of the camp. Behind the men of Honiton came the Puritan cloth-workers of Wellington, with their mayor upon a white horse beside their standard-bearer, and a band of twenty instruments before him. Grim faced, thoughtful, sober men they were for the most part clad in grey suits and wearing broad-brimmed hats. "For God and faith" was the motto of a streamer which floated amongst them. The cloth-workers formed three strong regiments and may have numbered close on six hundred men...

Peaceful farmland at Daisy Mount, near West Hill, just above the end of the Rockbeare straight.

   Behind them were musqueteers from Dorchester pikemen from Newton Poppleford and a body of stout infantry from among the serge workers of Ottery St Mary.

4 HONITON

Five miles due east from Larkbeare and at the logical conclusion of the old Roman road, stands the market town of Honiton. Famous for its lace industry and as a pleasant staging post on the carriage route to London, its taverns and hotels have housed many dignitaries, authors and nobility over the years. Charles Dickens stopped there after reporting on a case in Exeter, and Colonel Brandon and John Willoughby in **Jane Austen's** *Sense and Sensibility* (see page 134) both overnighted while travelling in the opposite direction. The town marks the beginning of the climb up into the Blackdown Hills which stand as the north eastern frontier of East Devon. From their top, looking west, a superb view of greater East Devon opens up. Virtually the entire Otter valley spreads out ahead - the flat-lands all the way to Exeter and the glittering sea coast from Exmouth almost to Sidmouth. The patchwork of green fields, the sudden tufted head of Dumpdon Hill, the silver streak of Exe estuary in the distance backed by the austere wall of Dartmoor hills, is a spectacular sight, especially in morning light.

It has to be this view, or one very like it, that greeted **Daniel Defoe** (1660-1731) during his lengthy perambulation of the nation, published as his *Tour*

DEFOE

26

through the Whole Island of Great Britain (1724-26). Defoe, an enigmatic but major figure in the canon of world literature, is widely considered to have written the first modern novel, *Robinson Crusoe* (1719). He was also a business man, traveller and spy for the English government. The latter came about after he wrote an ironic political pamphlet entitled *The Shortest Way with Dissenters* which landed him in prison. His only way out was to take the King's secretive shilling as a publisher of their propaganda. His Tour came towards the end of his life and his description of Honiton is probably the most rapturous account in the entire **Tour:**

> *I cannot but recommend it to any gentlemen that travel this road, that if they please to observe the prospect for half a mile, till their coming down the hill, and to the entrance into Honiton, the view of the country is the most beautiful landscape in the world, a mere picture; and I do not remember the like in any one place in England; 'tis observable that the market of this town was kept originally on the Sunday, till it was changed by the direction of King John. From Honiton the country is exceedingly pleasant still, and on the road they have a beautiful prospect almost all the way to Exeter, which is twelve miles...*

Such enthusiasm is obviously shared by the writer **Tom Fort**, although less for the panorama, than the way to it. ***A 303; Highway to the Sun*** (2012) illustrates very effectively how most people today take their tours through the island of Great Britain. It presents a highly personal account, or rather epic history, of the

FORT

27

FORT A303, a road well known to all East Devonians. For him the journey ends just inside the Blackdown Hills Area of Outstanding Natural Beauty (AONB), where the A303 merges into the A30. But for us Devonians, its expiry marks a beginning, as the two roads join together on the map like a blunted needle injecting the lifeblood of tourists, cars, vans and delivery vehicles into the county. But today its character as a narrow, single-carriageway road meandering through the Devon hills is increasingly troubled, thanks to the pressure of ever greater numbers of vehicle tyres hammering its tarmac – as **Tom Fort** observes:

> *Devon welcomes you as you reach the Marsh bypass… Beyond Marsh the A303's designation as a strategic highway to the west becomes absurd. There is a testing little hill which leads up to a 90-degree left-hand bend signalled in advance by a 20 m.p.h. speed limit sign. Twenty miles per hour! How is the mighty London-Penzance Trunk Road fallen! The sweet Devon air is filled with the dissonant hubbub of hissing brakes, grinding gear changes and straining engines as the trucks pant their way around the obstacle, hardly able to summon ten miles per hour, let alone twenty. The road's spirit does not recover. It limps up and along Sandpit Hill and crawls into Newcott… a bit of a non-place… The end is close. And it comes without even a whimper… There is no sense in the A303's sudden demise. It is done in swiftly and without fuss, by its old rival, the A30…* (From Chapters 16 and 17)

Dumpdon Hill and the edge of Honiton (far left), while descending from the Blackdown Hills. One of the several possible views described by Daniel Defoe.

After the A30 take-over, the road lunges down into East Devon, its lanes spreading out like capillaries from either side of the tarmac. To the left lie the quaint, but little-known villages of Stockland and Membury, to the right Upottery (where the poet **Patricia Beer** ended her days, see Chapter 11). Dunkerswell waits beyond that and further still, clinging on just inside the AONB, lies the highly picturesque village of Broadhembury. There, in what has to be one of Devon's most classic cob and thatch villages, lingers the spirit of the **Reverend Augustus Toplady** (1740-78). This essayist, author of the hymn *Rock of Ages* and early animal rights campaigner, saw out his short life as vicar of the high-towered 14th-century St Andrew's church1768-78.

Close by its fine Tudor pub, the Drewe Arms, derives its name from the local landowners, the Drewe family. Long established in the region, they would almost certainly have been familiar to **R.D. Blackmore** (1825-1900), the north Devon author of *Lorna Doone*. He set his less well known but similarly epic ***Perlycross, a Tale of the Western Hills*** (1894) in and around Culmstock, six miles north of Broadhembury, just two miles outside the EDDC border into the Mid Devon District Council (MDDC) administrative area. While not strictly East Devon, the novel's action is played out against the backdrop of East Devon's Blackdown Hills – the same 'Western Hills' of the title.

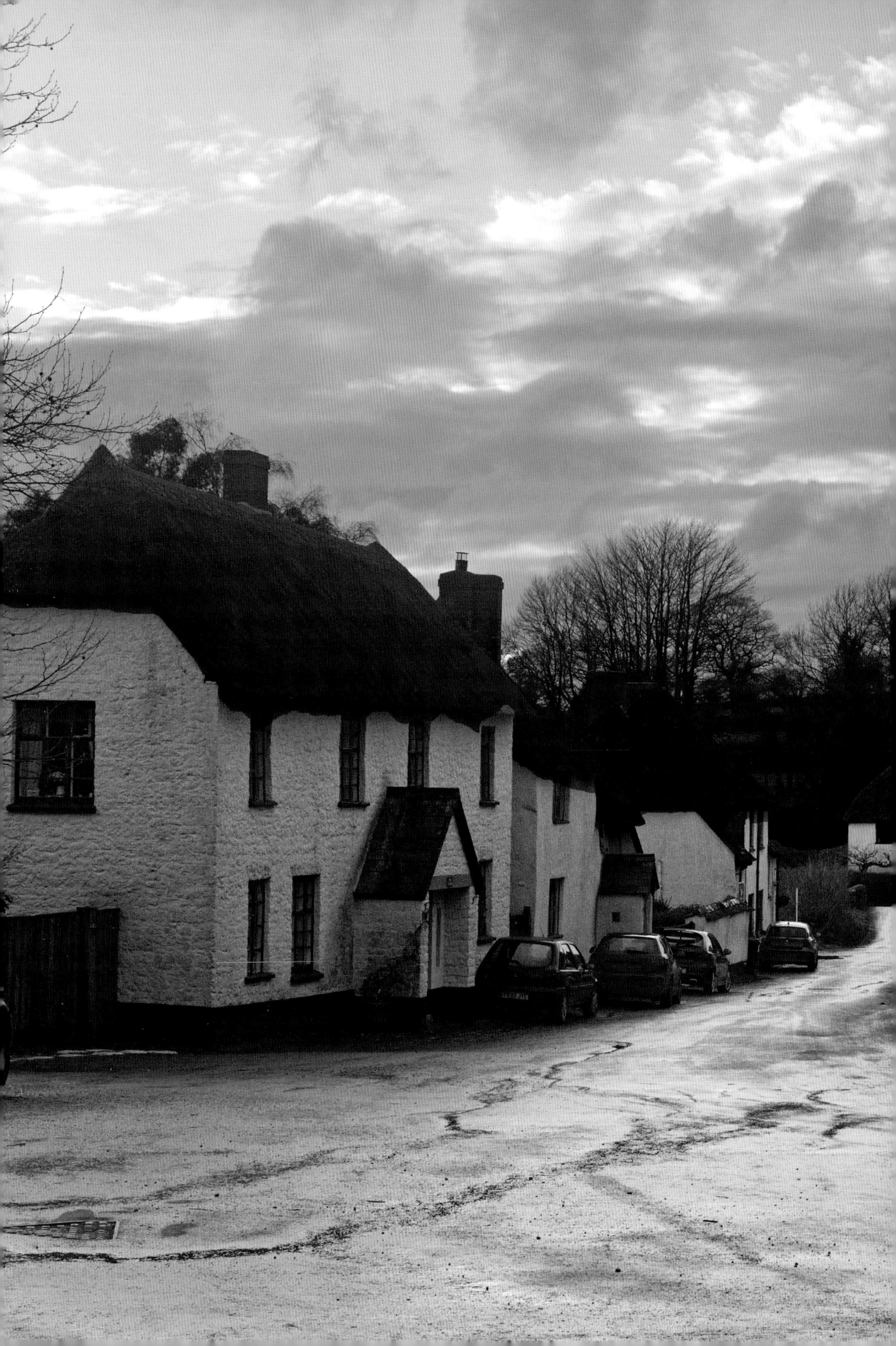

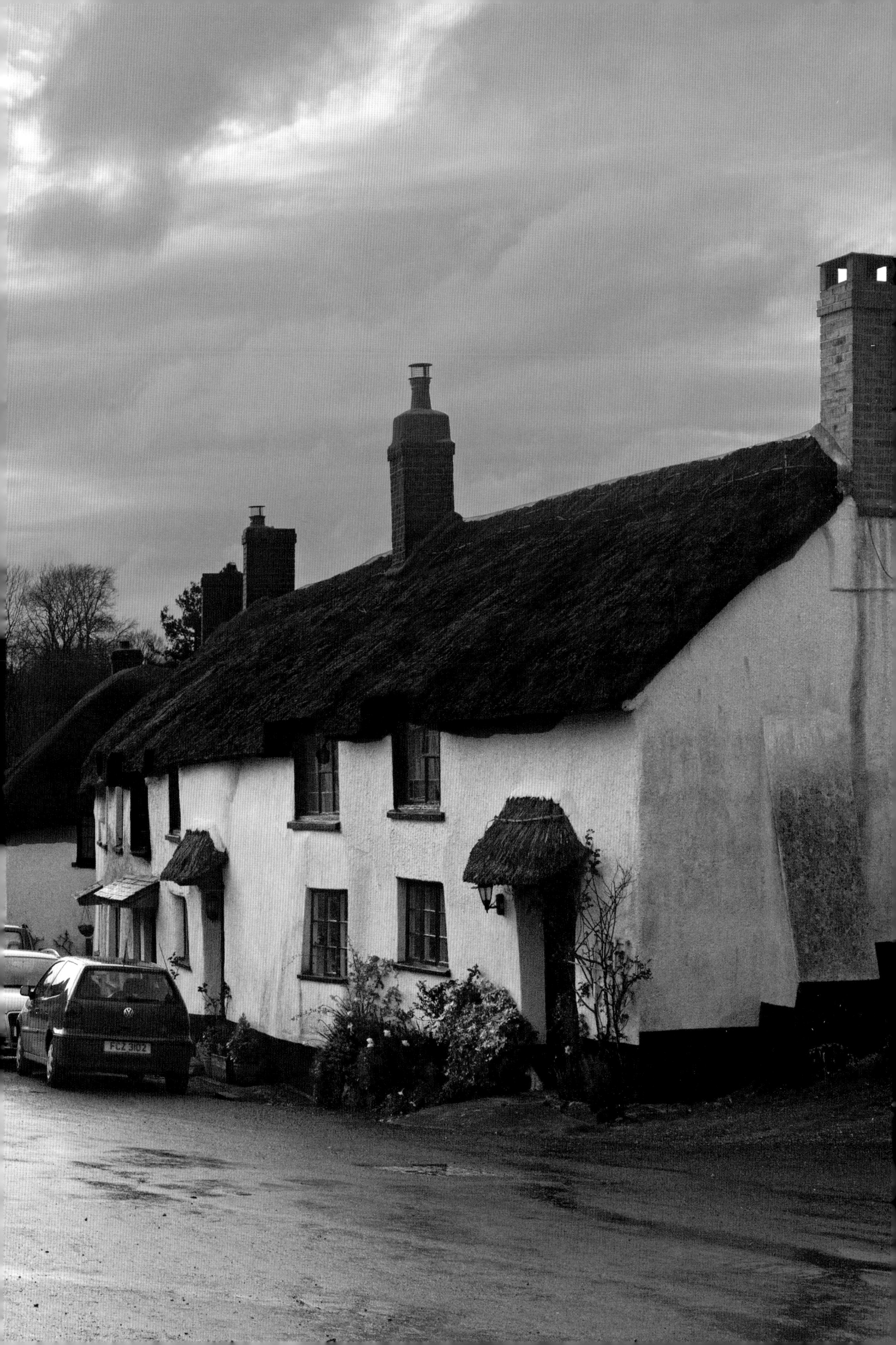
FCZ 3102

5 AXMINSTER and MUSBURY

PREVIOUS PAGE
Broadhembury, the village that hosted the hymn writer and early animal rights advocate, **Reverend Augustus Toplady** in the mid-18th century.

When travelling down by rail down from Waterloo, the arrival of East Devon declares itself as the river Axe sidling up beside the train a few miles short of Axminster. The transition from Dorset to Devon is seamless, but the wide Axe valley suddenly announces the presence of the sea as a destination in the mysterious empty space opening up due south. Some regard this as nature's placard proclaiming the arrival of the Southwest true. It is only here that the sea begins to earnestly force its presence inland via a sequence of river valleys, lining up one after the other all the way to the grand Exe estuary.

There is a theory in the town of Axminster that here might also mark the beginnings of England true – as a historic entity. It is said that somewhere in the surrounding landscape the crucial Battle of Brunanburh took place in 937AD. The event is claimed as the first victory for the English as a nation, when a force of Anglo-Saxons from Mercia and Wessex decisively defeated the alliance of Scots, Danes and Irish Norsemen at an, as yet, unknown location. **John Leland** (1503-52), 'the father of English local history,' who visited Axminster, mentioned the sight of a number of Saxon and Danish tombs side by side in the large church.

LELAND

He recorded it in his ***Itineraries*** (1538-43):

Famose by the sepultures of many noble Danes slain in King Æthelstane's time, at a battle on Branesdowne Thirby, and by the sepultures likewise of sum Saxon lords slain in the same field.

This is used as evidence of the battle, even if the tombs have unfortunately since been removed. On the strength of this it is worth mentioning **Alfred Lord Tennyson**, (1809-92) who came to East Devon with John Keble, the hymn-writer. The Poet Laureate made the first modern translation from the Old English poem in the *Anglo-Saxon Chronicles*. Entitled ***The Battle of Brunanburh*** (1880) and apparently much liked by Queen Victoria, it presents a stirring account of a very bloody victory.

If the area truly is the venue of a dramatic conflagration, it may be no surprise to discover that six miles away from the town exists one of Britain's most unstable and bizarre geological areas – the Seaton Undercliff. Spanning the six miles of shoreline between Seaton and Lyme Regis, the land seems to break all its own laws, becoming unreliable, even deceitful. In this dangerous section of the Jurassic Coast the ground's upper layers of chalk, sandstone and greensand appear as normal, but in fact can slip over a clay and limestone base toward the sea at any second. Undercliffs are one of the few genuinely uninhabitable areas of Britain's landmass and this is one of the largest in Western Europe. But

TENNYSON

of course human beings always try (including one of the writers covered in this book, as we will see on page 37). In the 1839 Bindon Landslip, sometimes called the Great Slip, a huge, three-quarter of a mile section abruptly slid seaward to create a new island boiling up out of the water. It also opened up giant chasms in the farmland, large enough to be harvested as separate fields. Victorians came from far and wide to view this eccentricity of nature.

19th-century engraving of the Bindon landslip. Shortly afterwards it became a significant tourist attraction.

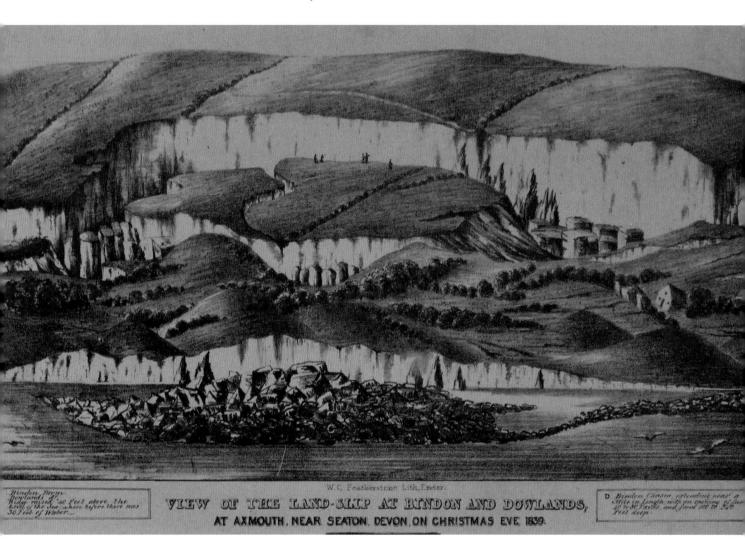

W.C. Featherstone Lith, Exeter.

VIEW OF THE LAND-SLIP AT BINDON AND DOWLANDS, AT AXMOUTH, NEAR SEATON, DEVON, ON CHRISTMAS EVE 1839.

However resting against this land-born madness lie the halcyon slopes of the Axe valley, which offer themselves up as supremely accommodating to the human dwelling. On their flanks, three miles south of Axminster, stands the modest village of Musbury.

It is to here, along a winding Devon lane that the poet, translator and detective story writer **Cecil Day Lewis** (1904-72) fled and set up home in 1938. Arriving just prior to the war, he would make it his intermittent base for the next 12 years. Like several other of Devon's 20th-century visiting writers, this former Communist, turned Poet Laureate (1968-72), came here mid-career, seeking the calm of the countryside, hoping to unravel some of the psychological complexity of his life, in his case abandoning his belief in 'the Party'. He describes his

DAY LEWIS

departure from Oxford in his autobiography *The Buried Day* (1960) with the sentence: *'I noiselessly slipped the painter… into a simpler world where wood and iron, grass and flowers and windy skies would renew a mind dulled by abstractions.'*

From a whitewashed, thatched cottage called Brimclose, surrounded by fields, hedges and Devon lanes, he accomplished his retreat from politics and role as a minor literary celebrity. He arrived at the time when there was even talk of an 'Auden-Spender-Day-Lewis school of poetry,' and his previous volume of poems *A Time to Dance* (1935), had been published by Virginia and Leonard Woolf's Hogarth Press. But engulfed by the rich green of the Axe valley, he quickly involved himself in another kind of complexity – human sensuality. Soon the lanes and hedges became scenes of covert assignations with a local farmer's wife. When that ended he took up with the writer Rosamond Lehman creating a bizarre ménage-à-trois with his wife, spending his time in a number of locations around England, as well as his *'little Paradise'* in Devon.

But while he learnt the art of creating a secret life within the Devon fields he generated another within his own profession. During this period of ostensibly working on his excellent translation of the *Georgics of Virgil* (1940), he was also developing a new career moonlighting as the detective story writer **Nicholas Blake**. From a desk deep in this Devonshire valley he would go on to write 20 novels, all but four featuring the private detective Nigel Strangeways, part modelled on his friend from Oxford, W.H. Auden. With titles like *The Beast Must Die* (1938): *Malice in Wonderland* (1940), they sold well and he was able to earn a reasonable living as a writer.

Looking down from the fields above Musbury it is easy to identify the house in which Nigel Strangeways lived. It can be done by reading the **Nicholas Blake** novel written around the time of his arrival, *The Smiler with the Knife*

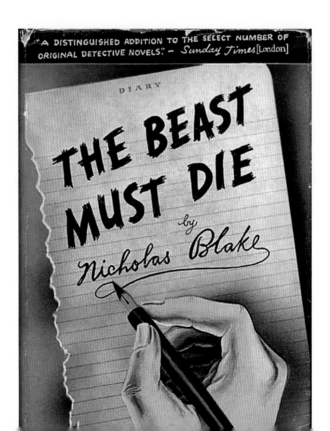

The hand that wrote *The Beast Must Die*, (1938) by C. Day Lewis's alter ego Nicholas Blake, spent a lot of its time in the house opposite.

C. Day Lewis's 'little paradise,' Brimclose overlooking the Axe valley. He arrived here in 1938.

(1939). In it we find the detective installed in an identical *'thatched, whitewashed cottage,'* precisely like Brimclose. He describes its setting as *'the lane from the village passed their cottage up over the brow of the hill, you could get to the sea that way after 5 miles of rough going…'*

Which fits exactly. The harbour at Lyme is about that distance. Furthermore, looking out from the house's upper windows over the village can be seen:

> *…the silver coil of the river in the valley below. Everything was peaceful. There was no sound or movement but the distant rattle of an express that hurried westward on the far side of the valley, white smoke laid across its back like an ostrich feather.*

This clearly is the railway line from Waterloo, passing along the Axe floodplain between Axminster and Honiton. Day Lewis would spend a good deal of time ensconced in this landscape as well as visiting the nearby towns and villages. His children's novel **The Otterbury Incident** (1948) is set in a small country town just after the war. It tells the story of two rival gangs from the local King's School. The fact that not-far-away Ottery St Mary's main school (see page 10) is also called The King's School and dates back to Walter Raleigh's time, makes it pretty clear in which direction his eyes strayed.

The plot may have been aided by his time of enlistment into the Home Guard from 1940. He served in a lookout, watching for signs of a German invasion, thus joining that long tradition of East Devonians who scoured the sea for the next band of Vikings, French pirates, Spanish Armadas, or revolutionaries (such as the Duke of Monmouth, see page 24). This explains the region's remarkable number of Beacon hills. It also led to a poem in 1940:

DAY LEWIS

Print of the 1839 Bindon landslip, on display at Lyme Regis museum, originally sold as a souvenir for the Victorian tourists.

Watching Post

A hill flank overlooking the Axe valley.
Among the stubble a farmer and I keep watch
For whatever may come to injure our countryside -
Light-signals, parachutes, bombs or sea-invaders.
The moon looks over the hill's shoulder, and hope
Mans the old ramparts of an English night...

The farmer and I talk for a while of invaders:
But soon we turn to crops – the annual hope,
Making of cider, prizes for ewes. Tonight
How many hearts along this war-mazed valley
Dream of a day when at peace they may work and watch
The small sufficient wonders of the countryside.

VIEW OF THE LANDSLIP AT WHITLANDS NEAR LYME REGIS.
About One Mile to the Eastward of the Great Chasm at Dowlands, which took place on the 3rd Feb.y 1840

To the Inhabitants & Visitors this plate is most respectfully inscribed by their very obedient servant, Daniel Du

UPLYME and the Underclif 6

The treacherous ground of the Undercliff, as described above, has served as an instinctive lure for writers. While several have been tempted to write about it, like **Peter Benson** in his **The Other Occupant** (1990), none have actually lived in it - except for one.

The start of the road leading to **John Fowles's** (1926-2005) East Devon home carried a sign stapled to a tree. It stated the way was currently closed. But this didn't chime with the couple of fresh tyre tracks leading out of puddles straight ahead towards Ware's Coastal Path. Continuing cautiously on foot for about three hundred yards along the route came a clue: a section of newish tarmac with dramatically jagged tears on an oddly dipping surface. The left side of the road seemed to have suffered a severe subsidence, dropping at least a foot below the right side, and recently.

The map indicated that Fowles's house, Underhill Farm, stood just inside the landslip area slightly below Ware, now a Nature Reserve. He had moved to this remote, deeply rural spot with his wife Elizabeth during his 'escape to the country' in 1965, just after finishing his novel **The Magus** (1966). Finding a building that spread out a full view of the sea and with a thick, tangled wood behind, he set about creating his next book. He composed the novel's plot while walking, bird-watching, flora and fauna studying in the area. He once even went native in the Undercliff for a period of two weeks (October 1966) in *a strange symbiosis with nature [in which] I became an element of nature myself.'* Of that time he wrote in a letter to his friend Denyse Sharrocks, that the nearby sea *'roars, pounds, hisses, mumbles on the reefs below our fields all day long, and then all night gives a sort of voice to all those powers of nature that are exterminated almost everywhere else in England… Green men could survive in those impenetrable thickets.'*

The voice that he heard would generate the book that many believe is his best and certainly most successful **The French Lieutenant's Woman** (1969). This remarkable historical novel set in 1867, but written by a narrator speaking from the psycho-analytically savvy, late 20th century, was transformed into an Oscar-nominated film starring Meryl Streep in 1981. As a result, the nearby Lyme Regis Cobb (the ancient, rounded harbour wall) where his heroine famously stood staring out to sea, found itself promoted around the world. This is all thanks to the sentences pounded out in that wooded, far-eastern corner of East Devon.

Some sixty pages into the text Fowles paints a vivid portrait of the Undercliff as a kind of counterbalance to the extreme Victorian gentility dominating the town of Lyme Regis set directly below:

FOWLES

37

FOWLES

... its deep chasms and accented by strange bluffs and towers of chalk and flint which loom over the lush foliage around them like the walls of ruined castles... its enormous ashes and beeches; its green Brazilian chasms choked with ivy and the liana of wild clematis; its bracken that grows seven, eight feet tall; its flowers that bloom a month earlier than anywhere else in the district. In summer it is the nearest this country can offer to a tropical jungle. (Chapter 10)

Back on the path, the search for Fowles's house threw up another curiosity. How had such a landscape reacted to the effects of his pen and home-making nearly fifty years earlier? Two hundred metres further along the trail came the first clue: the sight of a totally collapsed house on the edge of a thick, tangled wood. The walls had buckled, the bricks imploded, the rusted roof lay torn and useless at various angles. But directly beside it stood a neatly maintained wooden shack, allbeit leaning like a Crazy-House, surrounded by a lovingly tended garden. Such an incongruous contrast: a capsized, overgrown farmhouse graced by a mowed lawn, trained bower arch, a tidily parked motorcycle. A moment later a man appeared in the shack's doorway asking in a Scottish accent, if any help was needed.

Could this by any chance be Underhill Farm, where John Fowles lived between 1965 and 1968?

'Yes it is…' he replied, gesturing towards the pile of twisted bricks, capsized walls and bent roof.

The place he wrote **The French Lieutenant's Woman**?'

The windows installed by **John Fowles** in his writing house at Underhill Farm.

'He wrote it in here,' he gestured to the leaning shack out of which he had just stepped. Responding to several looks of deepening curiosity he added, 'I live here now.'

But the house pitched so precariously forward, as if pulled towards the sea by a huge magnet; surely it could go the way of its neighbour at any second? Not, one would have thought, the venue for a sound sleep. Did it make collapsing noises at night?'

'Yes,' he answered calmly, 'it's a kind of rumble. The house moved about an inch last week.'

Certainly an act of true dedication to a home and the memory of one who lived there before. Fowles had initially found his rural isolation an inspiration, although he reported suffering from frequent nightmares, one in particular returning again and again, of a *'strange, sallow-faced woman.'* Clearly this had some bearing on the germination of his forthcoming novel's main character, Sarah Woodruff, the French Lieutenant's woman. A quick glance inside the shack revealed the large window that Fowles had installed to use as the mental canvas on which to compose his text. But the floor below it was about a metre lower than the same floor beside the entrance. The repaired floorboards made a steep but graceful curve down into the main room. Furthermore the large, plate-glass window had just, a couple days earlier, received a long crack, from one side to the other. Without doubt the slipping ground on which Fowles wrote was slipping again, possibly as fast as in 1968 when one morning he stepped out into the garden only to discover a whole row of trees in his familiar sea view no longer there. Overnight a several acre section of fields had simply moved on down towards the shore, its trees *'ravaged and split'* the bushes *'somersaulted.'*

But by then his book had been created. And it wouldn't be long before the earth moved again under Fowles's feet, but this time in terms of his career.

FOWLES

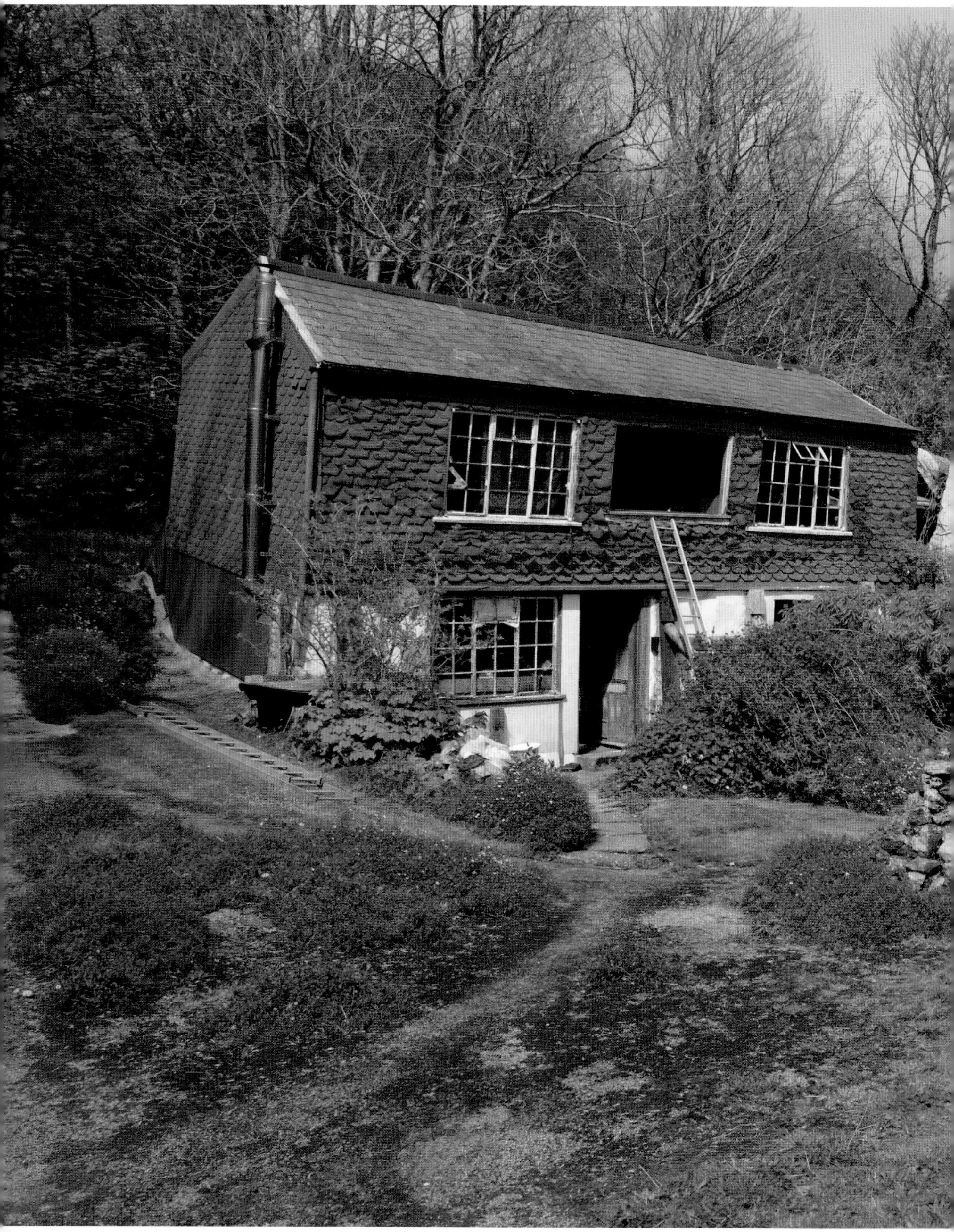

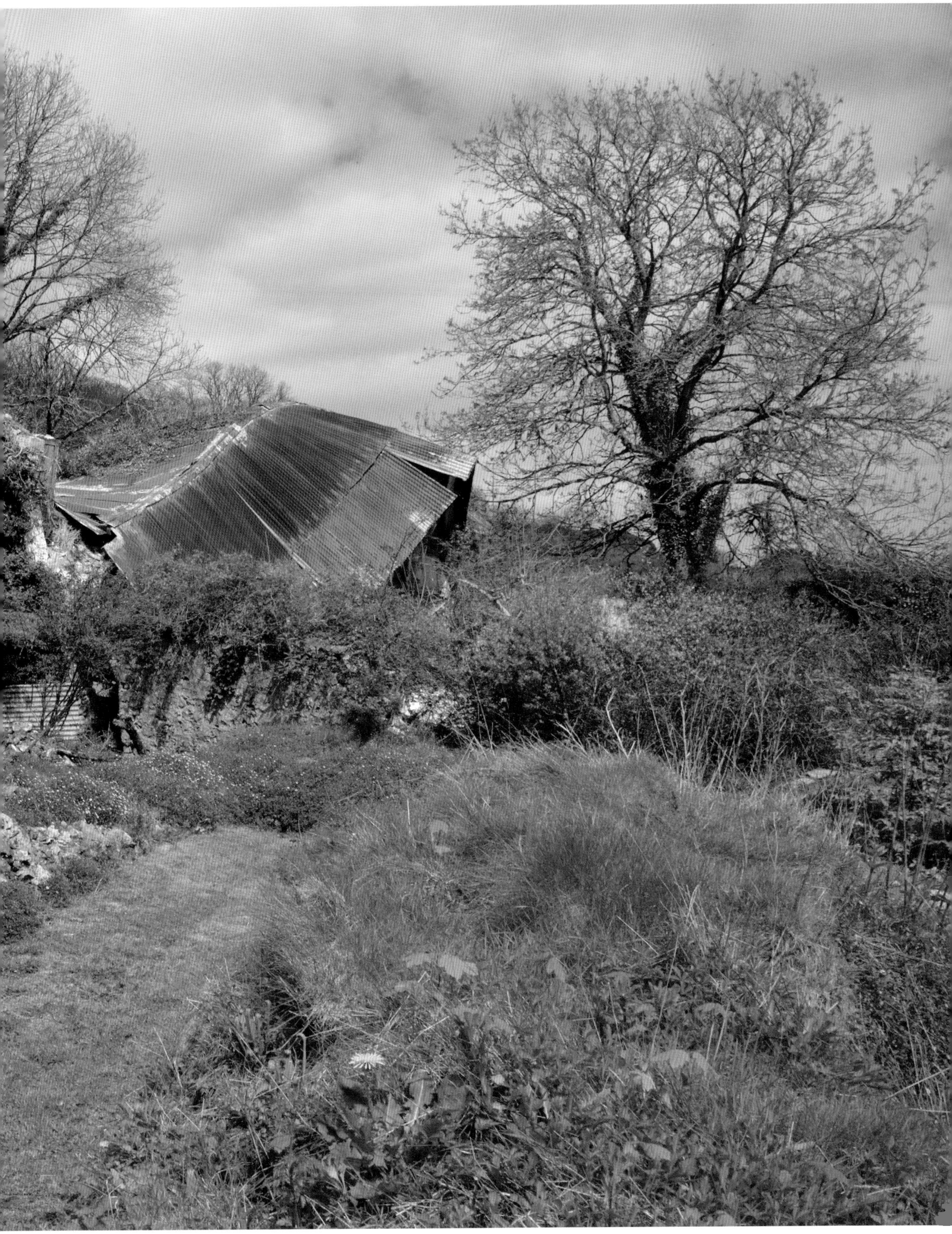

The French Lieutenant's Woman's huge international success enabled him to buy the elegant Belmont House a mile east in Lyme Regis itself (Dorset), away from the slipping chalk and greensand of the Undercliff.

But who then was Underhill Farm's current and almost certainly last tenant? Did he by chance ever meet the great writer?

'Yes, I tended his garden for 20 years.'

The words were stated matter-of-factly, as if inhabiting Fowles' writing house, continuing to tend his garden was a completely natural response to the memory of the writer who later, as Curator of the Lyme Regis Museum, campaigned so hard to preserve the area's historic character and ambience.

In his novel, Underhill Farm carries a strong presence as the 'Dairy'. Not far away is the spot above Pinhay Bay on Ware Common where the other main character, Charles, discovers Sarah Woodruff alone and asleep on a naturally created cliff-top bed of grass, surrounded by anemones. The place where he stared and contemplated this solitary woman whose huge sadness had so captivated him on the Cobb. The very spot in the landscape where her eyes popped open and their gazes met; at which moment moment Fowles says:

in that luminous evening silence broken only by the waves' quiet wash, the whole Victorian age was lost.

She walks away, but he follows her and then experiences her face as a thing that *'seemed to envelop and reject him; as if she was a figure in a dream, both standing still and yet always receding.'* It is hard not to make a connection with *'the sallow-faced woman'* reported in letters, that appeared in his nightmares early on during the novel's gestation at Underhill Farm.

Then, almost as if he wants the reader to know this, seven pages later he suddenly breaks away from the narrative to address us directly, declaring:

FOWLES

...if this is a novel it cannot be a novel in the modern sense of the word. So perhaps I am writing a transposed autobiography; perhaps I now live in one of the houses I have bought into the fiction; perhaps Charles is myself disguised...

The fact is he did live in one of his fictional houses. The Dairy, as described, was Underhill Farm. Its location, *'slightly below the path'* after *'a break in the trees'* of Ware Common woods; its shape *'long;'* its position, with *'two or three meadows around it,'* confirm this. Whether he was Charles is another matter. But either way this is a fine example of a writer trying to crack open the very process of writing. To offer up the event of himself as creator, sitting in the actual environment that he describes, writing those words staring out at the empty horizon beside the East Devon Undercliff. Most of the authors in this book have done the same; but Fowles invites us up very close, actually into his writing shed. In a later book **LAND** (1985), created with the photographer Fay Godwin, he speaks about his own relationship to landscape. *...what I seek myself in landscape... is the personal and direct experience of it, above all, the flowing and unfixed experience of it.*

There can be few less fixed places than the Undercliff. He goes on to address the frequent mis-interpretation and romanticising of landscape that *'hides the reality of what is going on there,'* particularly the use of its farmland:

Ever since people grew sentimental about the countryside and its landscape, it became a source for provoking emotion, a gymnasium for the sensitive, [so] it has become more and more difficult to be honest about it. It has become too convenient, too lucrative for the majority of artists not to distort it, to beautify, to soften, make elegant, to garden it to suit public taste.

Fowles, a writer from the 1960s, deliberately chose the dangerous and unstable Undercliff as the venue in which to end the Victorian era of repression for his characters. There beside that jungle of giant ferns, green 'Brazilian' chasms, just about anything could happen. Indeed once, in his writings about the Lyme area, he proudly mentioned the fact that *'two escaped German prisoners of war... survived there for three years during the war.'*

Fortunately for us it was in this place that he came of age as a writer. As he puts in his loosely autobiographical **The Magus,** he left his English university with *'a third class degree and a first class illusion – that I was a poet... but I did absorb a small dose of... Oxford's greatest gift to civilised life; Socratic honesty.'* Surely the wild, unmolested nature of East Devon helped him give it full application.

To experience the Undercliff for oneself, take Walk 3 – set out on page 49

7 SEATON and BEER

AUSTEN

East Devon's Undercliff, with its shifting sandstone on clay surface, stretches six miles along the coast from Lyme Regis to the Axe estuary at Seaton. The image of an unpredictable and unstable ground beneath the action of human life is the kind of metaphor writers love. Even **Jane Austen** (1775-1817), whose description of landscape is famously understated, found herself carried away in her depiction of the Pinhay section of the Undercliff in **Persuasion** (1816):

> *...the woody varieties of the cheerful village of Up Lyme, and, above all, Pinny [Pinhay] with its green chasms between romantic rocks, where the scattered forest trees and orchards of luxuriant growth declare that many a generation must have passed away since the first partial falling of the cliff prepared the ground for such a state, where a scene so wonderful and so lovely is exhibited, as may more than equal any of the resembling scenes of the far-famed Isle of Wight: these places must be visited, and visited again...*

The temptation to place the action of a novel on its surface is understandable, as John Fowles did (see previous chapter). But for a full-blown opera of human emotion staged on the Undercliff one might look to the **Reverend Sabine Baring Gould** (1834-1924).

An early engraving of the Reverend **Sabine Baring Gould.** Artist unknown.

Writer of over 40 novels in a stirring, slightly over-blown language reminiscent of his hymn 'Onward Christian Soldiers,' famously written in 15 minutes, this Devon folklorist, song-collector, hymn-writer and prolific author, (born in Exeter but living mostly at Lew Trenchard near Okehampton) set one of his more vivid works of fiction on the Seaton Undercliff. **Winefred, A Story of the Chalk Cliffs** (1900) is a tale of love, smuggling and human treachery, timed to coincide with the Undercliff's cataclysmic Great Slip of 1839 (see image on page 33), which features prominently at the book's climax. Furthermore the novel is written with the kind of biblical verve that places the imagery of nature at the centre of the plot, as much as any book of the time. Below is its opening:

*One grey uncertain afternoon in November, when the vapour laden skies
were without a rent and the trailing clouds without a fringe were passing
imperceptibly into drizzle, that thickened with coming night; when the land
was colourless and the earth oozed beneath the tread, and the sullen sea was*

View of Lyme Bay from on top of the Seaton Undercliff. Most of the time it is deceptively tranquil.

BARING GOULD

45

as lead – on such a day, at such a time of day a woman wandered through Seaton, then a disregarded hamlet by the mouth of the Axe, picking up a precarious existence by being visited in the summer by bathers.

The woman drew her daughter about with her. Both were wet and bedraggled. The wind from the east soughed about the caves, whistled in the naked trees, and hissed through the coarse sea-grass and withered thrift; whilst from afar came the mutter of a peevish sea.

…I and my Winefred are homeless. My cottage has gone to pieces, and the whole cliff is crumbling away. The wall is down already and the lime-ash floor is buckled and splitting. No one now may go nigh the place. It needs but the hopping of a wagtail to send the whole bag of tricks into the sea. (Chapter 1)

Winefred's mother's cottage had been built on the Undercliff, which was moving again. The landscape had begun literally swallowing it up. Thus opens the action of a super-charged plot that races forward to make the first 80 pages of **Winefred** into what might be called a thunderous good read, even if the modern reader might spot the odd cliché and plot simplification.

In his day Sabine Baring-Gould was often compared to and outsold Thomas Hardy (1840-1928) and R.D. Blackmore (1825-1900) author of *Lorna Doone* (1869). But he always rated his novels as inferior to his book of west-country folk songs **Songs of the West** (1889) which he painstakingly researched, mostly in the taverns and inns across Devon and Cornwall. Later he collaborated with Cecil Sharp to make **English Folksongs for Schools** (1906). However as a by-product of his musical research he created his **Devonshire Characters and Strange Events** (1908). This book contains a number of true stories from the west country including an account of the smuggler Jack Rattenbury from the East Devon village of Beer (described in **Winefred** as ' *a village of fishermen, but every fisherman was suspected of being a smuggler').* He borrows Rattenbury's real name for a character in **Winefred,** and in his depiction clearly shows a sympathy for the impoverished coastal and agricultural workers of 19th-century south Devon. Indeed he married a factory-worker from Yorkshire, Grace Taylor, who is rumoured to be the model for Eliza Doolittle in **George Bernard Shaw's** *Pygmalion.* Shaw had been a visitor to their house in Lew Trenchard and showed great interest in their exogamous marriage.

But in terms of literature and landscape this novel is a full-blooded example of human emotion blended with the emotions of nature – as if both exist as adjuncts to each other. The text fairly brims with the anthropomorphic and reverse anthropomorphic imagery:

Finally came a burst of yellow flame. She had kindled the candle and this she at once placed in the lantern. Not only could he see the walls of the chasm, the flint stones glinted in it like eyes. (Chapter 13)

BERNARD SHAW

Poster from 1903 advertising a guide to Seaton and Beer. Note the reference at the bottom to Jack Rattenbury, the smuggler whose memoirs were borrowed by Baring Gould.

The landscape is looking back at human beings with its own eyes. Not long afterwards the ground begins sliding horribly under the house of the main characters, and with a vengeance reminiscent of the *Book of Revelations*:

> At once was seen a jagged fissure running like a lightning-flash through the turf, followed by a gape, an upheaval, a lurch, then a sinkage and a starring and splitting of the surface. In another moment a chasm yawned before their eyes, three quarters of a mile long torn across the path, athwart hedges, separating a vast tract of down and undercliff from the mainland, and descending down into the bowels of the earth... the depth contained a tossing mass of crumbled chalk and erupted pebble, with occasional squirts of water, some two or three hundred feet below the surface on the land side. It was like a mighty polypus mouth that had opened and was chewing and digesting its food in its throat and belly. (Chapter 49)

BARING GOULD

BARING GOULD

Such passages raise that much contested question: 'Does nature possess its own emotions?' While the moods of the natural world are traditionally ascribed to the controlling God or local deities, poets and novelists often give the impression that it does. This can happen even if they themselves don't believe it, simply because the nature of language forces them to use words whose very images belong to the surrounding air, ground, local vegetation. Baring-Gould rarely shies away from a stirring adjective. His character's feeling might be described as *'tempestuous,' 'sunny,' 'wet,' 'thunderous.'* At one time he says of his young Jack Rattenbury, *'the young spirit is like young wheat- it grows weak, watery, yellow, where there has been overmuch rain, overmuch cold. All it needs is the sun.'*

The reading of **Winefred** readily provokes questions into the nature of emotion itself. Although the feeling response was well instated into the human psyche long before the arrival of language; the moods of nature, its 'ragged sky,' 'trembling earth,' 'stormy sea,' would inevitably form verbal counterparts within the human brain. We and the ragged sky have evolved together; our bodies are wholly nature dependent and our minds, with the new-fangled facility of language, merely following behind.

Winefred is a tale in which nature itself appears to pass judgement on the chief villain. The land is even portrayed as possessing a mouth and a belly (see the excerpt above), which literally devours him. But the effectiveness of this nature-born description is shown by the popularity of **Sabine Baring-Gould's** novels. His *The Red Spider* (1887) went into nine editions, *The Broom Squire* (1896) thirteen.

And his process of writing them is also interesting. Usually he made a single two or three week visit to the location he wished to describe, but never

Souvenir print of Beer Head from the mid 19th century. Note how far the coastal erosion has progressed from the photograph opposite.

took notes. Returning home he would then write the story out at great speed, all the descriptions taken purely from the impressions burned into his memory. Revision apparently was minimal. Thus we receive a vivid, intuitive response to landscape. For this reason the 'voice of nature' that emerges in his work is far clearer and more powerful than his future critics gave him credit.

Walk 3 - John Fowles   *The Undercliff*

It is possible to walk the entire distance of the Undercliff following the well-marked West Coastal Path between Seaton and Lyme Regis (about seven miles). At the Seaton end it starts just over the river Axe at the Axe Cliff Golf Course. At Lyme Regis it climbs up the cliffs from the town centre to the large car-park. At this point it picks up the Coastal Path and continues past the remains of Underhill Farm before diving into the heavily wooded Undercliff National Nature Reserve. The walk is fairly demanding and one is not advised to deviate from the path into the 'jungle,' which surrounds it about 80% of the way. The famous 1839 landslip area is now heavily overgrown and hard to view. There is no proper access to the sea. Most people only walk the beginning sections at either end and return the way they came. But there is a bus between the two towns for those who want to experience the full 'Brazilian' wildness as Fowles did. Fowles wrote his own guide books to the area which can be found at Lyme Museum.

Beer Head today, with the former restaurant at Branscombe beach in the foreground.

8 BRANSCOMBE

TORRANCE

Around the white chalk headland, and one bay along from the former smugglers' haven of Beer, lies the smaller, less nefarious village of Branscombe. Spread out pleasantly along the bottom of a steep valley, like many pirate-fearing coastal settlements, its centre conceals itself from the sea. The way to the shingle seashore involves a pathway through a wide open grassy field, as it has for centuries. Fortunately the village's character has been well preserved and is carefully tended by its inhabitants, including the former university lecturer and poet **John Torrance** (1933-):

> ### On Branscombe Beach
> *Spent surf slides growing back down the shingle*
> *but over the next wave's head, before it breaks,*
> *flings up a shawl of white lace.*
> *Again and again and again.*
>
> *Those lace-making girls of long ago,*
> *if they stole an hour on the beach with the boys,*
> *would have hated this grudging voice of the shingle*

and the waves like so many grumbling grannies
in white lace shawls, all bellowing
"Back, you trollops, go back!
Get back to your bobbins and pillows!"

However, life is not always idyllic in the coastal valleys. In 2007, a twist of fate caused by a storm off the Lizard in Cornwall, brought the smugglers pouring back to the beaches at Branscombe and Beer. The container ship the MSC Napoli, operated by a company registered in the British Virgin Islands, had started to sink out in the English Channel. Its crew were hurriedly winched off to safety but after the storm the ship remained afloat, although crippled. Tugs were sent to pull it to Portland Harbour for salvage, but half way there the body of the hull began to show signs of failure. Before it snapped the hulk was beached on a sandbank a mile off shore at Branscombe. It wasn't long before the contents of the containers started to be washed up along the shore.

Those wishing to avoid paying Her Majesty's excise (or in fact anything) took advantage of this latest bounty from the sea. They descended on the villages of Branscombe and Beer in cars, vans and trucks, scavenging whatever the sea decided to offer up, then hurried away with their trophies – from BMW motorcycles, to perfume, to nappies. Eventually the police had to cordon off the beach. But of course wreckings on the Devon and Cornwall coasts used to be relatively common – depositing not only goods, broken masts and hulls on the beaches, but also sailors (see **Orlando Hutchinson's** painting on page 83). Below is a reaction to the Napoli's demise by Sidmouth resident **Robert Crick** (1944-):

CRICK

Cargo

Broken-backed behemoth with a flag of convenience
Crashing through the oceans with a skeleton crew,
And a cargo of cat food,
Nappies and motor-bikes,
Foil-wrapped biscuits and a training shoe.

Wreckage of the Napoli, rusting on a sandbank,
Luring loads of grockles to the local bars,
With containers full of globalised
Anti-ageing moisturisers,
Empty wooden barrels and some big posh cars.

Poisonous polluter on the Heritage coastline
Killing off the coral and the breeding birds
With a cargo of nickel bars,
Bibles, drive-shafts,
Personal possessions and sump-oil turds.
(2008)

But inland from the shore exists another completely different world, the kind not seen by tourists and scavengers. Still in the Branscombe area, the Beer based novelist and poet **Rowland Molony** (1946-) applies his pen to the kind of farmland scene in winter from which most people turn. Set at roughly the same time of year as the Napoli wreck, the atmosphere captured in the land is no less evocative.

Borderlands

Amber cloud-light spills out from under a late December afternoon.
A freezing sun slides down behind the blackened tree-networks,
and over field-acres stolid pigs are ambling perimeter wires.

Above them squadrons of birds peel up and away from the mud wastes,
they rise and fall in the cold dusk airs; they light onto the suck
of slop-wallows, iced shitpools where pigs trundle their bow waves.

The pigs rub wads of gristle against each other, their punchbag bums,
their rows of baggy teats, earflaps, horny noses, - through the swill ponds,
they lever up stones and set awash gouts of silt-creamed waters.

MOLONY

The failing light is filled with crows and gulls, a whirl of starlings;
along the field hedge stark oaks are studded with rooks in the branches.
Where is salvation for these creatures under the stain of spent light,

under a draining sky, the comfortless onset of winter's night?
The land is peeled; birds cling to the stalks of trees; pigs wade the wasteland.
Here is Outside. Regions where a thought dare not go. Borderlands

Looking towards
Beer Head from the
end of the Esplanade
at Sidmouth

9 BRANSCOMBE and WESTON

POTTER

Continuing up the cliff path away from Branscombe towards Sidmouth, one soon enters a steep wood that in early summer transforms into a sea of wild garlic. The trees seem to sprout from a surface of tossing white flowers. The path continues upward, carving its way through the thick aroma until suddenly emerging onto the top and a wide open plateau. Here the closeness of the sea-mist and sky combine with the emptiness of fields to create a delicious new sense of freedom. The friendly pastures go on and on, extending right over to the cliff edge, inhabited by fearless rabbits – which were also loved by another well-known writer who liked to walk this way around the turn of the 20th century.

Strolling along the top towards Weston, catching glimpses of the remote beaches far below, we can easily blend the images of her work with Darwinian ideas of animal life evolving from the sea onto land, then up into human–beings. Certainly a gift to anyone inclined to satire, with its opportunity of reversing evolution; transform the human-being back into the animal from whence it came.

While the process is achieved easily with language, using simile – 'he/she looked like a mouse/dog/fox/pig/duck' etc, only a very few writers have been able to

Wild garlic in the woods above Branscombe village, along the path probably followed by Little Pig Robinson.

Little Pig Robinson on his way to market from the book *The Tale of Little Pig Robinson* by **Beatrix Potter**. He follows the path along what looks like the Weston cliff top.

physically illustrate their text better than the reader's own imagination. **Beatrix Potter** (1866-1943) is definitely one such. Her coloured drawings of Peter Rabbit (1901) and his friends, are a delight the world over, and not only for children. Originally created merely for her own pleasure, then sent as pictorial letters to children, it is often forgotten that one of her earliest animal inspirations was not just rabbits hopping along cliff-tops and other such venues, but also pigs. *The Tale of Little Pig Robinson* (1930) was written the same year as Peter Rabbit's publication (1901), but wouldn't see print for another 29 years. Interestingly for us, it is set in the town where she wrote it while on Easter holiday that year – Sidmouth (she stayed at Hylton House on Seafield Rd). This, the last in her Peter

A walker's signpost on the cliff top close to Weston, the possible location of the above drawing made by **Beatrix Potter.**

Drawing from *The Tale of Little Pig Robinson*, as he begins his journey to Stymouth. Note the thatched mill building in the background.

Rabbit series, tells the tale of young Pig Robinson's first big venture alone out into the wide world. His journey begins with an epic walk across the East Devon landscape to the market at 'Stymouth,' where his adventures truly begin. It is along these same cliff tops that he, (and therefore she with him), clearly walks.

In a letter from November 1941 **Beatrix Potter** admitted Stymouth to be Sidmouth, but with additions. The harbour is closer to Teignmouth and Lyme Regis, the steep streets, Ilfracombe. But even so the river Sid receives an even more unflattering name – the Pigsty. At least one of the drawings is recognisable as Sidmouth's Church Street, although filled with busy, frocked piggies, dressed up cats and bowler-hat wearing chickens. The cliff meadows close to Weston are fairly recognisable, as is a stile that she sketched while in Sidmouth; a copy of the original is on display in Sidmouth Museum.

Many claim **Beatrix Potter** as one of our most brilliant satirists. She escapes censure because the texts of her popular Peter Rabbit series follow the logic of children not adults. Grown-ups happily laugh off her plots as giantly improbable and 'kids' stuff.' Indeed Little Pig Robinson, after setting out for market with a basket of eggs and cauliflowers, ends up in the land of the Bong Tree.

The Mill at Uplyme photographed in the 1920s. See the strong similarities with the drawing above. Today a hedge and trees block this view.

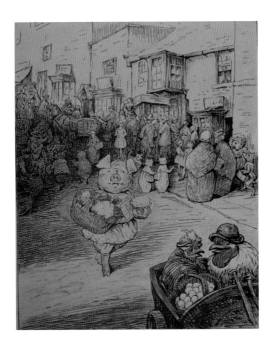

Pig Robinson arrives in Stymouth from *The Tale of Little Pig Robinson*. The street carries strong similarities to Sidmouth's Church Street.

But who cannot sense something hauntingly familiar in her frock-coated piglets and bonneted geese?

Clearly she wrote the pig story while still discovering and experimenting with her style. She aimed this story at slightly older children as is suggested by its more descriptive nature. But again it is possible to trace the places in the landscape from where the ideas flowed.

Little Pig Robinson's adventure begins with a long, four mile journey from Piggery Porcombe Farm across the Devon countryside down the cliffs, across the 'Styford bridge' (surely today's Sidford) to Stymouth. She describes the town as *'clean, pleasant, picturesque, and well-behaved (always excepting the harbour).'* Again some of the drawings are recognisable. The mill at Uplyme is unmistakable as are the open fields by Weston. As he goes, clutching his basket of eggs to sell at the market, the adventurous little pig's senses are awakened by:

the dark blue sea… yellow pussy willow catkins in flower… primroses in hundreds on the bank, and a warm smell of moss and grass and steaming, moist red earth.

It is a route that can be done today, see **Walk 4** below, if the Uplyme Mill, and Styford bridge are missed out. But the now restored Mill can be seen in **Walk 5**, although not as Beatrix Potter drew it, because trees and a new hedge have sprung up blocking her view. Both walks are superb in very different ways and best done in the imaginative company of the author. Often real rabbits and sometimes pigs, will help the process. But while the little pig's journey belongs to the realms of fiction, anyone who takes the real walks should definitely keep their eyes well-peeled for the *'important rooks, lively jackdaws… vicious old cows.'*

POTTER

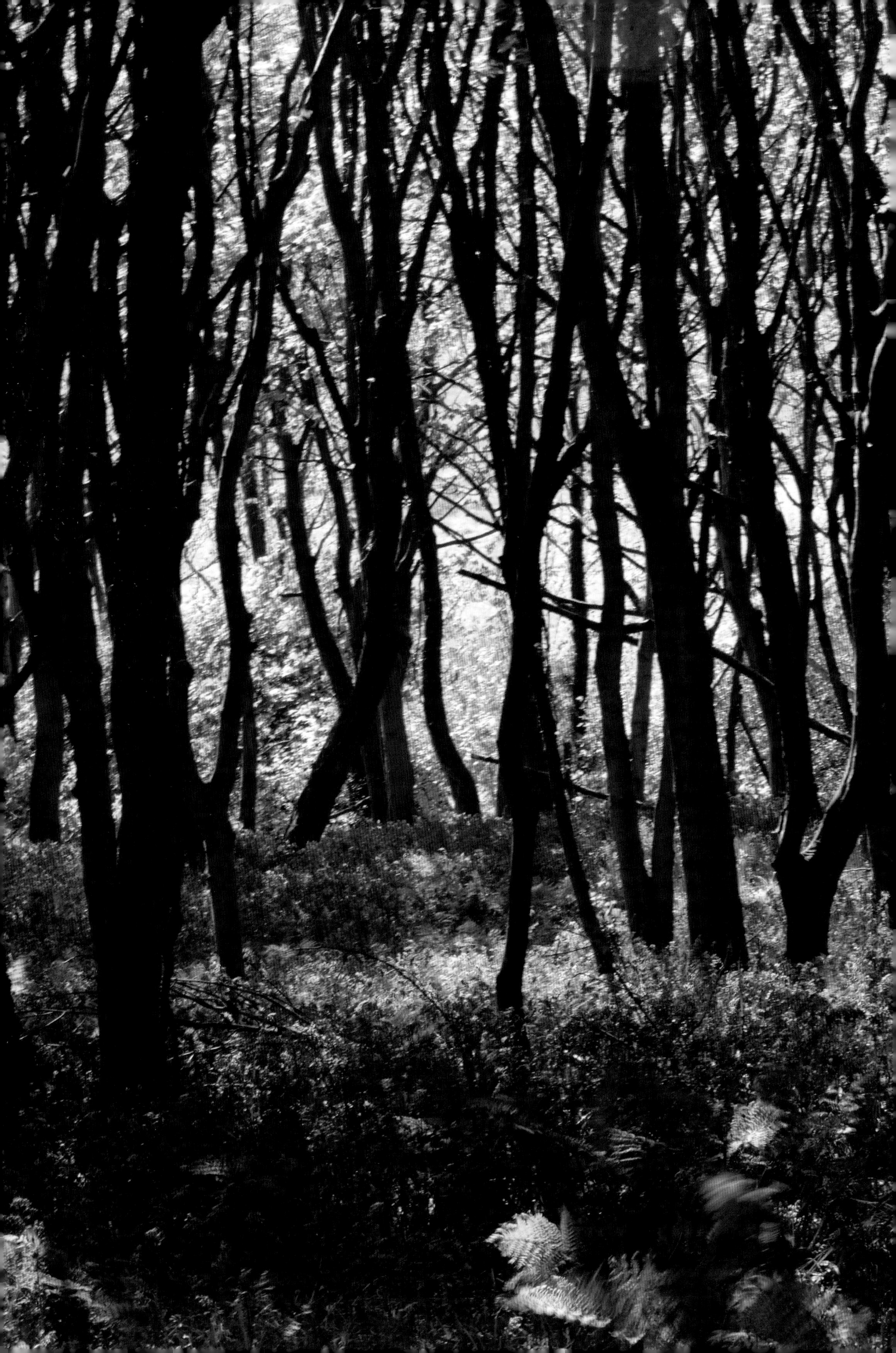

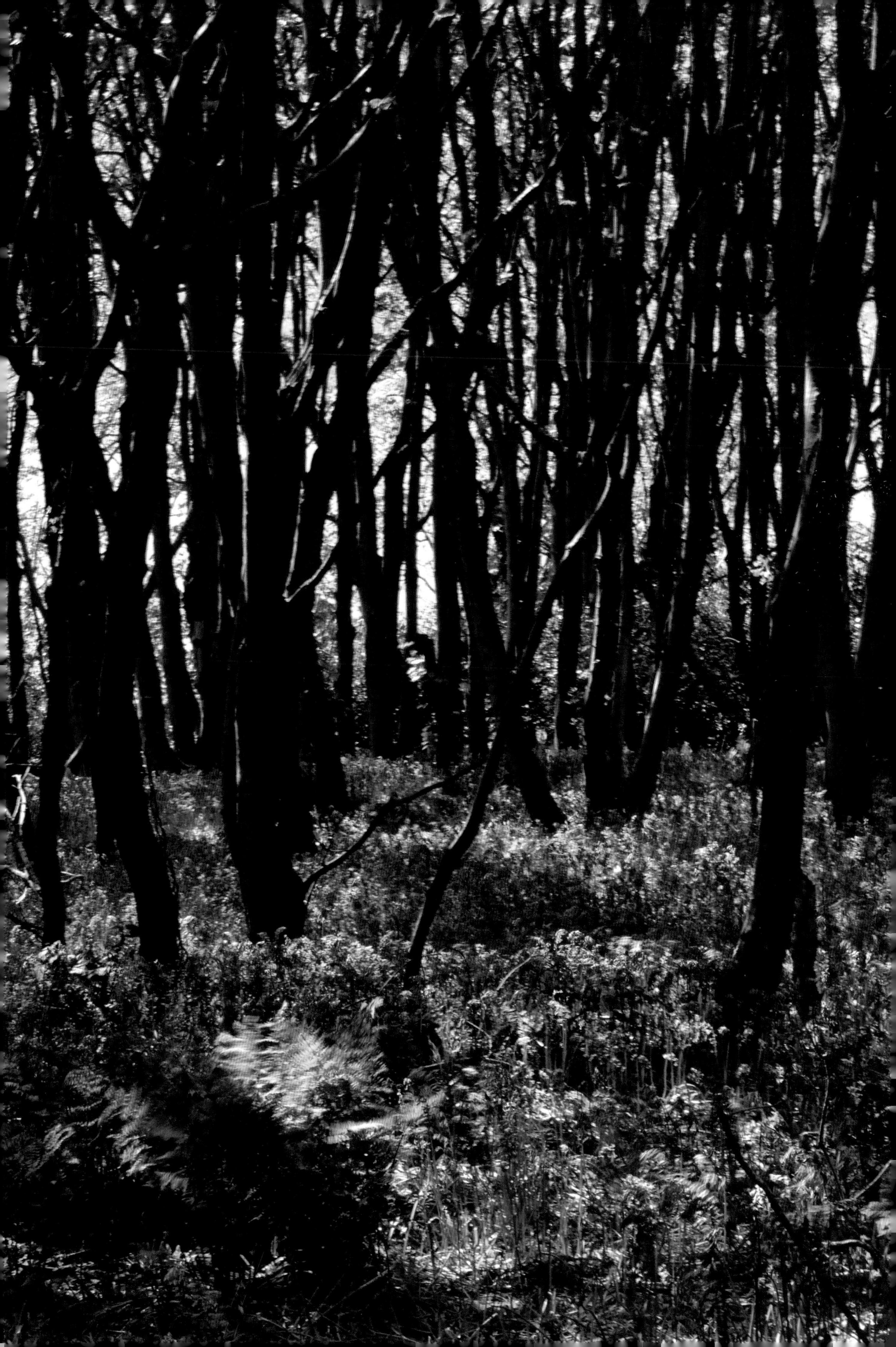

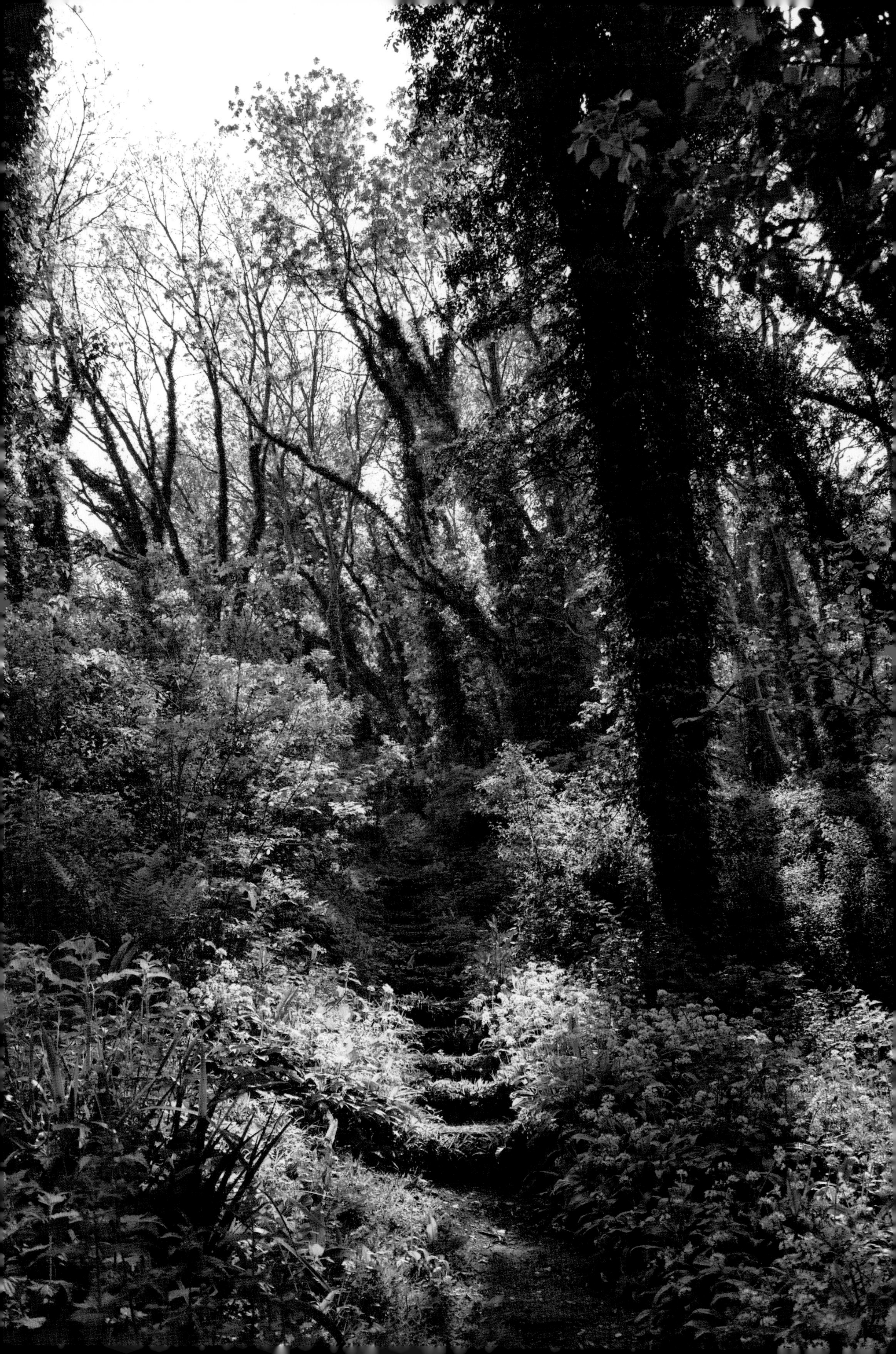

Walk 4 - Beatrix Potter   *Branscombe to Sidmouth*

To follow Little Pig Robinson to market at Stymouth, several possible starting points offer themselves. But since Beatrix's Potter's actual route clearly involves poetic licence, so can ours. Her drawing of Robinson crossing the bridge in front of Uplyme Mill in her Chapter 3, indicates one starting point. But that gives the little pig a massive 16 mile hike with basket full of eggs and cauliflowers. Far more practical and enjoyable is to believe Aunt Porcas's estimation of the distance at 'four miles if it's one.' In this case a good clue for a starting point comes from her coloured drawing showing Robinson strolling happily along a cliff-top meadow near what looks like Weston Cliff up above Branscombe village. This place has a fine atmosphere and it is easy to imagine Beatrix Potter halting here, inhaling the air and quickly pulling out her sketch book. Her coloured drawing shows the little pig walking through a friendly pastoral seascape set high above the water, slightly sheltered from the wind but in sight of a deep blue sea. The walk is easy to find simply by taking the cliff path climbing up from Branscombe beach and following it all the way to Sidmouth. About five miles in total, it is well-trodden and marked, containing two significant 'ups,' one at the start from Branscombe beach, the second two thirds along at Salcombe Regis. The end involves a steep descent through the heavenly bluebell-scented woods (if in May) down to Sidmouth.

Walk 5 - Beatrix Potter   *Lyme Regis to Uplyme*

Walk up from Lyme Regis (in Dorset) along the river (or 'rivulet') Lyme to the Mill at Uplyme (in East Devon). The way climbs gently for slightly over a mile and is well marked. A simple but beautiful walk, also done by Beatrix Potter herself, with sketchbook, when holidaying in Lyme Regis. She stayed at Burley, Silver Street in April 1904. The sharp whitted may query why this 1901-written story contains drawings from 1904. But Potter re-shaped and expanded the original story just prior to its publication in 1930.

PREVIOUS PAGE
Bluebells in the woods just below the summit of Salcombe Hill, Sidmouth. Part of Little Pig Robinson's possible route to Stymouth.

Typical East Devon farm gate, passed further on towards Sidmouth.

10 SIDMOUTH

Of all East Devon's attractions to the literary spirit, it is the Regency town of Sidmouth that has drawn the most authors. Developed in the late 18th and early 19th century as a sea-bathing resort, it was then preserved as such by the fortuitous creation of Britain's oldest civic society, The Sid Vale Association in 1846. Its little-changed sea front flanked by two giant red sandstone cliffs, Peak and Salcombe Hills, still harbours the kind of sea-born calm that writers love.

A very good introduction to this atmosphere of the town can be found in the work of **John Betjeman** (1906-84), a great campaigner to preserve Britain's heritage and also Poet Laureate (1972-84). He held a special affection for the town and visited it several times, describing it in a BBC broadcast on 27th September 1949:

BETJEMAN

*A silver mist of heat hung over Sidmouth when I came into it. A silver mist
was over it when I went away. The climate is so dominant in Sidmouth you
can almost touch it. In Connaught Gardens – a modern piece of Italian-
style gardening on a cliff top, with a view through arches of red cliffs five
hundred feet high – sheltered from the sea breeze, plants would flower
and flower as high as the cliffs themselves if only the wind would let them.
For that is one of the first things I noticed about Sidmouth. As soon as
I was out of the gentle sea breeze I was in a hothouse where wonderful
West Country bushes filled the air with scent, and enormous butterflies lit
on asters and on antirrhinums, themselves twice as large as life. Fuchsia
bells seemed three times the size of those anywhere else in Britain. If it
were not for the sea Sidmouth, I thought, would be tropic forest. Devon
hills protect it on all but the seaward side. Peakhill and Salcombe Hill
guard the town west and east. Woods and little Devon fields climb their
slopes. Other hills, blue-wooded, rise far inland. And here is the little valley
of the River Sid – a brown moorland stream which disappears in shingle*

BETJEMAN

63

BETJEMAN

by the site of the old gasworks (now a car park)…I doubt if anywhere on the south coast there is a prettier Georgian stucco crescent than Fortfield Terrace which overlooks the cricket ground and sea…The crowds are neither vast nor noisy. No giant wheels nor kursaals intrude, no pier takes iron strides into the sea. The roads to Sidmouth are twisty, and the streets of the town are far too narrow even for private motors to move with ease, let alone char-a-bancs.

From ***Betjeman's Britain,*** (1999) created by his late daughter Candida Lycett Green.

Betjeman was a regular contributor to the *Architectural Review* and contrary to common beliefs, didn't just champion old architecture. First he sought to define the relationship between the building, village or town, and its setting. For this he applied his superb poet's eye to identify character within the surrounding geology, trees, streets, flowers before deciding whether to apply it to his journalism and campaigning. The effect is a lesson to all who seek to save our historic environment (it is largely thanks to him we still have the splendid St Pancras Station). He campaigned on all fronts, creating the Victorian Society and with his daughter Candida, set up the '*Nooks and Corners*' column in *Private Eye*. It was here that Sidmouth found itself again in 2012, owing to one of the many attempts to over-develop the town – the local District Council's proposal to convert a good section of Sidmouth's picturesque Knowle park (given to the Council by the people of Sidmouth for protection) into a housing estate. This aroused the ire of the usually accommodating local population who on the 3rd November 2012 marched out in force holding '*Save Our Sidmouth*' banners, in the largest demonstration in the town's history. It also produced strong reactions across Britain from Sidmouth's many admiring visitors.

The Mass March along Sidmouth Esplanade in November 2012 organised by the '*Save Our Sidmouth*' campaign.

One of the campaign's driving forces, **Michael Temple** (1936-), former Head of English at Exeter School, member of the East Devon Alliance (EDA) and the Community Voice on Planning (CoVoP), makes a call from the East Devon countryside with his Betjeman tribute poem:

Slough Revisited

John Betjeman, we need you now;
The country soon will be like Slough;
There'll be no grass to graze a cow -
All built upon.

The Planning Laws and Councils feed
The hungry mouths of builders' greed -
And they don't build for social need -
It's all a "con".

But let us all join hand in hand
From Axe to Tweed and make a stand
To save our green and pleasant land -
With your help, John.
(2014)

The Knowle gardens Sidmouth, part of which were put forward for development by the District Council (the owner), including a large section of this photograph. After a long, hard campaign by locals, the Council's Development Management Committee rejected their own application in March 2013.

TEMPLE

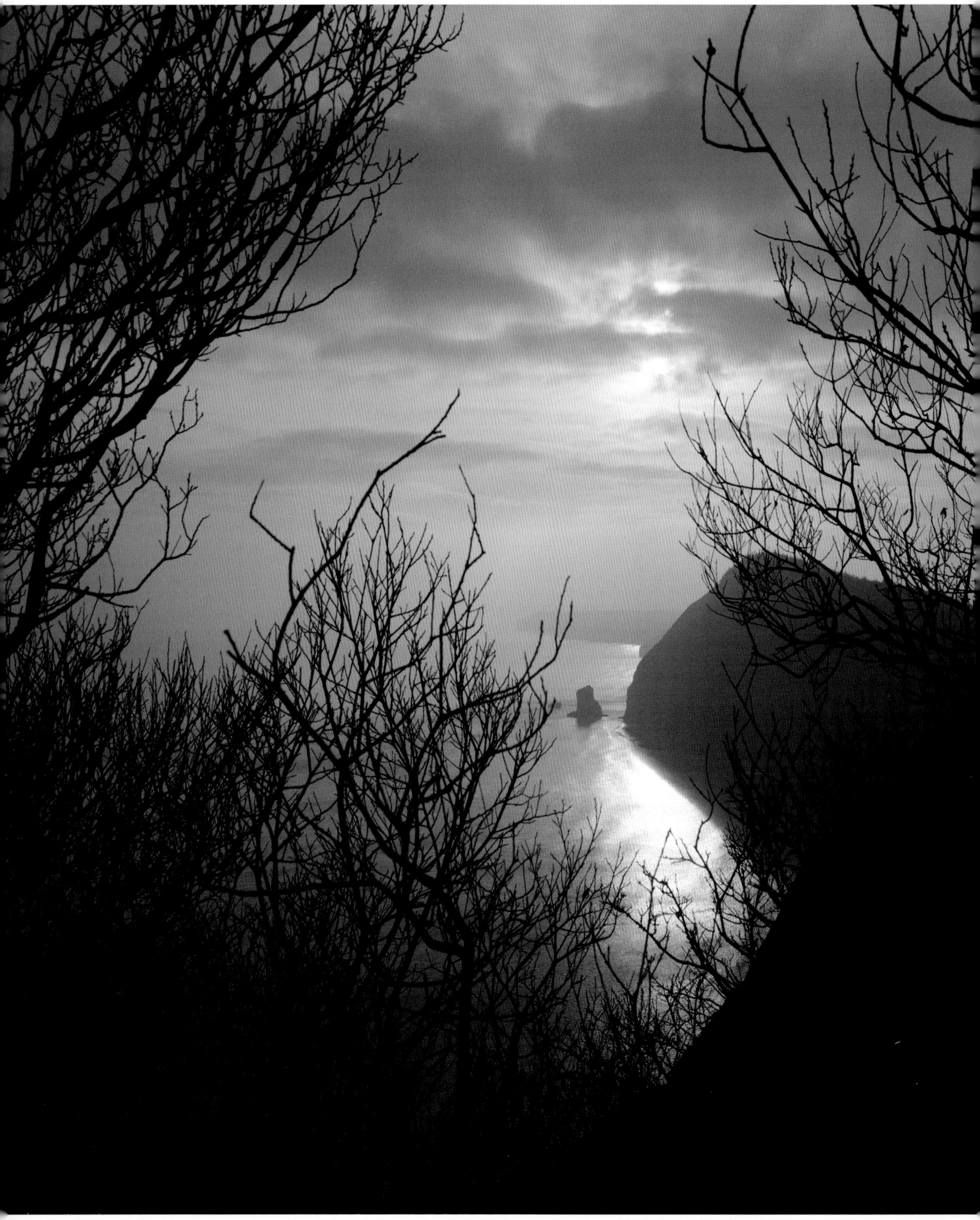

For a clue as to how the literary imagination can interact with East Devon's magnificent Triassic shoreline, we could do a lot worse than take a walk along the cliff tops between Sidmouth and Ladram Bay (see the cover photograph) at low tide, imagining oneself the young **H.G. Wells** (1866-1946). As he negotiated the path over the top of Peak Hill in March 1895, then down into the rolling farm lands, he would have received sudden glimpses of the dramatic red sandstone stacks at Ladram, the exposed seaweed, its long, glistening tentacles laid out on the low-water rocks. It is also quite possible he'd have spotted birds flustering over a human body washed up on the rocks from one of the surprising number of wrecks on this coast in the 19th century. **Orlando Hutchinson** – see page 83 – recorded that in 1838 '*around August four vessels were wrecked and all on the beach at the same time*'. Either way, under what he later described as an '*incandescent sky*' this sight would definitely have inspired a closer look. If so it might have revealed some sinister shaped seaweed among the '*wave worn rocks.*' In such a fantasy scenario it can't be discounted that these rocks may even have been Sidmouth's Chit Rocks as sketched and coloured by **J.M.W. Turner** in 1824, (see next page), if at the beginning or end of his walk.

Having placed oneself in the writer's shoes, it isn't difficult to switch into the shoes of the main character in his short story ***The Sea Raiders*** (1896), a retired tea dealer, who

> *…was walking along the cliff path between Sidmouth and Ladram Bay. His attention was attracted by what at first he thought to be a cluster of birds struggling over a fragment of food that caught the sunlight, and glistened pinkish-white. The tide was right out, and this object was not only far below him, but remote across a broad waste of rock reefs covered with dark seaweed and interspersed with silvery shining tidal pools…*

At this point in the process of composition, he might also have taken take a boat between the two beaches at high tide to catch glimpses of the seaweed's slippery arms floating and swaying under a boat's hull, reaching up towards the passengers. Again, remarkably easy to picture them as possessing '*large intelligent eyes.*' With his mind primed by the gothic fantasies from the likes of Edgar Allan Poe (1809-49), or Mary Shelley's *Frankenstein* (1818) someone like Wells could hardly fail to imagine them as the arms of an ogre-like, luminescent sea monster that temporally invades the coast of East Devon. The kind of creature with a penchant for devouring a few human bodies before vanishing back into the depths of the Atlantic.

However as a man very much of his time and unlike his literary predecessors Wells came to his profession fuelled by a passionate love of science. Keen to

OPPOSITE
View towards Ladram Bay from near the top of Peak Hill, Sidmouth.

Joseph William Mallord Turner's coloured drawing of Sidmouth's Chit Rock shortly before it collapsed in 1824.

advance the genre away from the seductive dreamscapes of Poe, he added an important note of scientific credibility. Thus he produced the opening line:

Until the extraordinary affair at Sidmouth the species Haploteuthis ferox was known to science only generically…

Haploteuthis ferox is of course fictional – at least so one hopes from the way the story develops – but the East Devon in which it manifests, is most real and certainly the generative source of the story. Wells describes the walk and its environs in some detail, so one can sense a strong imaginative involvement in this beautiful stretch of coastline into which the novelist's mind then dived. **The Sea Raiders** is one of Wells's earlier stories, written around the same time as *The Time Machine,* so might be considered as part-responsible for the birth of 'scientific romance,' or as it was later termed - 'science fiction,' for which he is credited.

Today the giant Otter sandstone cliffs around Sidmouth are part of the 95-mile long Jurassic Coast, which in 2001 received the status of England's first, and still only natural World Heritage Site.

WELLS

Fortunately this part of the East Devon coast still remains fairly similar to the landscape Wells knew – one of the few places covered in this book still able to make such a claim. Partly for this reason some have proposed nominating the coastal area for National Park status, in an attempt to protect it from the furious development that has been ripping through East Devon during the early 21st century.

Wells was just one of many sufficiently captivated by a landscape to insert it directly into their work. In Sidmouth the feature that serves as the strongest lure has always been the sea itself. Furthermore this sea-town is, unusually, without a harbour, being dominated instead by a long, gracious Esplanade that extends between both cliffs. It is punctured time to time by the River Sid that exits under the Alma bridge on its eastern end. The Sid's departure into the sea is a poetic feature in itself as it frequently decides to conceal its extinction into the English Channel by disappearing under the shingle bank for a month or so, giving walkers an uninterrupted stroll from cliff-end to cliff-end. The empty, sea-breathing Esplanade first thing in the morning, is a superb venue to witness the blending of human enterprise with infinity. But it is not only poetry that drew the crowds. In the Regency and Victorian era sea-bathing became a fashionable activity to promote health and mental vigour. Gradually the fishing boats dotted along the Sidmouth sea front were replaced by bathing-machines. As **John Fowles** (see page 37) writes in **ISLANDS** (1978) *'For many decades Sea bathing remained what it had been to Jane Austen, a medicinal activity'* and due to the injurious effects of the sun, *'the fashionable months… were October and November; one had at all costs to preserve one's ability to blush.'*

Bathing machines on Sidmouth sea front around 1880-90, as they steadily replaced the fishing boats.

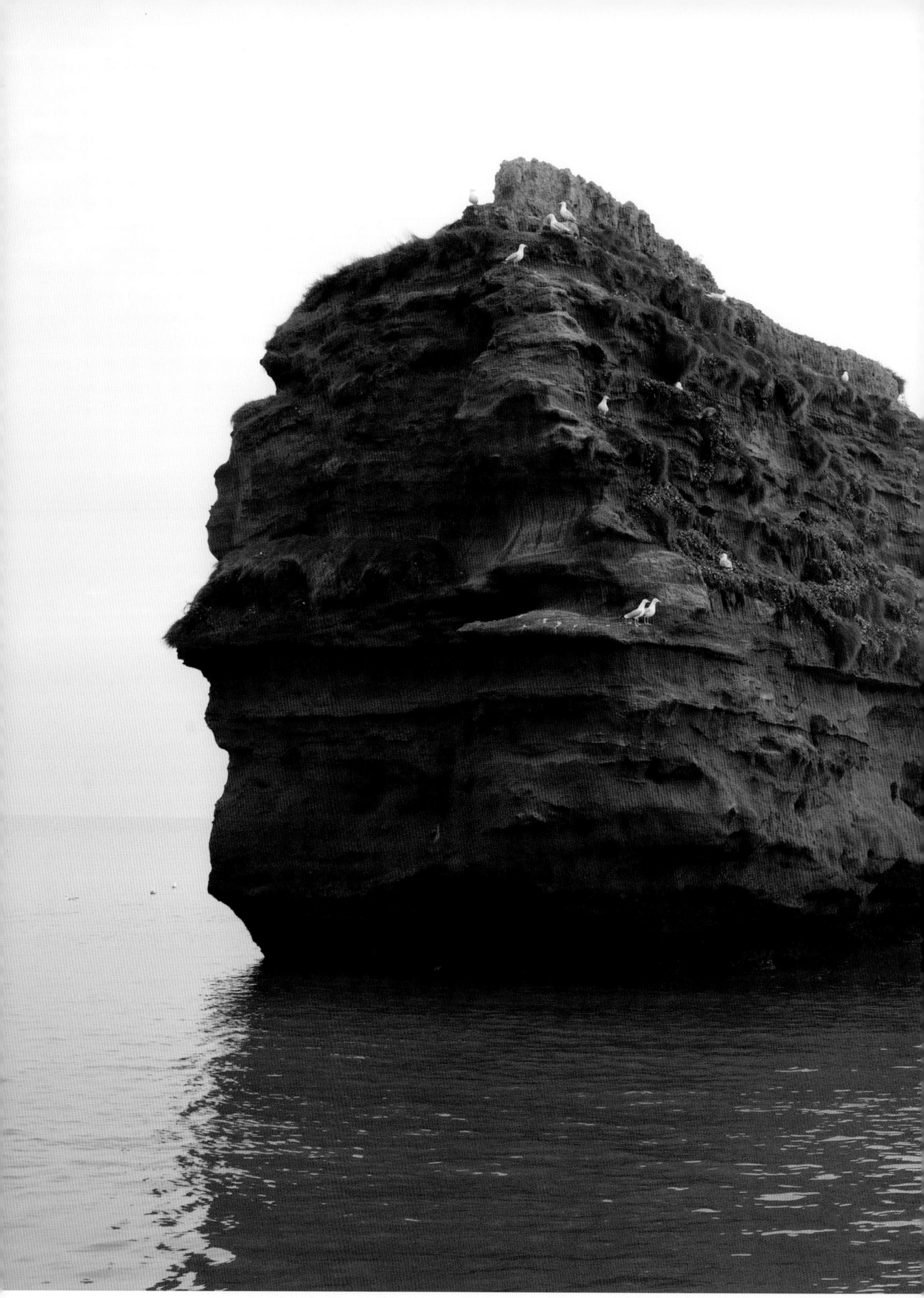

One of the Otter sandstone stacks at Ladram Bay, similar to the one painted by Turner, see previous page. These are among the best Triassic period stacks in the UK and one of the richest sources of fossil samples from between 200-250 million years ago in the world. The red colour is due to the oxidisation of iron in a landscape which at that time was near desert.

Elizabeth Barrett Browning, who was described by her husband Robert Browning as 'my little Portuguese.'

One such person who initially came more for the bathing (and blushing) than the poetry was **Elizabeth Barrett Browning** (1806-61). Brought by her father during their family's downsizing after his finances suffered a setback, she arrived at the age of 26, already weakening in health. Indeed her condition was one reason for the choice of the seaside. But it wasn't long before she picked up on the delicious sea-borne atmosphere - as she put it in a letter on her initial arrival at Rafarel House, Sidmouth (now 8 Fortfield Terrace; photo page 86) in August 1832:

The drawing room's four windows all look to the sea and I am never tired of looking out of them. I always thought that the sea was the sublimest object in nature. Mont Blanc… Niagara must be nothing to it. There the Almighty's form glasses itself in tempests… and not only in tempests but in calm… in space, in eternal motion, in eternal regularity.

Soon the sea with its endlessly shifting, moody surface was inspiring her pen. In those days she was simply **Elizabeth Barrett** as she wouldn't meet her great love, fellow poet Robert Browning until 1845. The literary zeitgeist coursing through the drawing-rooms of middle and upper-class England at the time came from the late Romantic poets (hence her reference to the 'sublime'). She would spend the next three crucial years of her poetic development looking out at the sea from various houses in Sidmouth. But the whole atmosphere of the town and its surroundings captured her imagination, as can be seen from the following letter extracts:

BARRETT
BROWNING

We came to Sidmouth for two months and you see we are still here; and when we are likely to go is as uncertain as ever. I like the place, and some of its inhabitants. I like the greenness and the tranquillity and the sea; and the solitude of one dear seat which hangs over it, and which is far too lonely for many others to like besides myself.

We live in a thatched house with a green lawn and bounded by a Devonshire lane. Do you know what that is? Milton did when he wrote of 'hedgerow elms and hillocks green.' Indeed Sidmouth is a nest among elms; and the lulling of the sea and the shadow of the hills make it a peaceful one. But there are no majestic features in the country. It is all green and fresh and secluded; and the grandeur is concentrated upon the ocean without deigning to have anything to do with the earth.

Letter to Miss Commeline 22nd September 1834

While this may not be **Elizabeth Barrett Browning's** actual 'lonely' seat; could it be the position? It is encountered just below High Peak on the path to Ladram bay (see **Walk 8** on page 81). Sidmouth lies in the background.

CARRIAGE APPROACH TO KNOWLE COTTAGE.

THE LODGE TO THE REV? M? HOBSONS.

Published Nov? 10? 1815 by J Wallis, Marine Library, Sidmouth.

It is scarcely possible, at least it seems to me, than to do otherwise than admire the beauty of the country. It is the very land of green lanes and pretty thatched cottages. I mean the kind of cottages that are... with verandas and shrubberies and sounds of the harp or piano coming through the windows. When you stand on any of the hills that stand around Sidmouth, the whole valley seems to be thickly wooded down to the very verge of the sea, and these pretty villas to be springing from the ground almost as thickly as quite as naturally as the trees

A selection of prints of Sidmouth's cottages orné, as on display at Sidmouth Museum. Most were built around the beginning of the 19th century and, save for the first, (Knowle Cottage), still exist. Sidmouth is said to have one of the best collections in the UK.

SIDCLIFF COTTAGE SIDMOUTH.
J. Bacon Esq?

CLAREMONT VILLA. SIDMOUTH
Commanding a fine Marine View.

*themselves. There are certainly
many more houses out of the
town than in it, and they all
stand apart, yet neat, hiding
in their own shrubberies, or
behind the green rows of elms
which wall in the secluded lanes
on either side. Such a number
of green lanes I never saw and
some of them quite black with
foliage where it is twilight in the
middle of the day, and others
letting in beautiful glimpses of
the spreading healthy hills or of
the sunny sea.*

Letter to Mrs Martin,
27th September 1832

CLIFF COTTAGE.
(Major Gray)
Pub.d by J. Wallis R. Marine Library, Sidmouth Feby. 1st 1826

CLIFTON COTTAGE.
(The property of E B Lousada Esquire)
Published by J. Wallis R. Moor Library Sidmouth

The work begun in this environment would result in its author being considered for Poet Laureate at the death of Wordsworth in 1850. But in the end she was pipped to the post by Alfred Lord Tennyson (see page 32). It was in Sidmouth that she composed her first mature poems as well as completed her initial translation of **Prometheus Bound,** which she later re-worked. Also the town was the last place she lived with full mobility before her already delicate health deteriorated to virtually confine her to an indoor life. But in Sidmouth, particularly along the flat, easy-to-walk Esplanade, she would have imbibed the full range of nature's moods along with the sea's engulfing presence, installing it solidly into memory.

Shortly after she left Sidmouth she published her first significant volume of poetry **The Seraphim and other Poems** (1838). One of its poems **The Sea Side Walk** is almost certainly set in the town, composed between the town's Esplanade and the Chit Rock (since disappeared, but painted by Turner, see on page 68), or, if the tide is out along the beach at Jacob's Ladder (see photo on page 73). It clearly shows her original vernacular style of verse starting to cut through the effusive wording inherited from the Romantics, as evidenced in lines 3-6 (for the poem in full see page 78). It was this distinctive quality of writing that would be developed by later poets like Emily Dickinson, whose bedroom wall carried a picture of **Elizabeth Barrett Browning.**

She left Sidmouth in 1835 to be installed in London, where not long afterwards she became more or less bed-ridden. Her affection for the town is revealed in a letter written later that year:

> …Half my soul in the meantime, seems to have stayed behind on the sea-shore, which I love more than ever now that I cannot walk on it in the body. London is wrapped up like a mummy in a yellow mist…

But her remarkable imagination would keep her engaged and alive, both in the mental endeavour of composing her increasingly original poetry and the physical attendance to her two great loves, her husband-to-be, the six-years-her junior Robert Browning, and her jealous spaniel Flush. She would write famous love poems to both, for which she is mostly remembered today. The first **To Flush, my Dog,** would a century later, inspire Virginia Woolf to write an entire novel in the guise of Flush's autobiography *(Flush)*. The dog of course served as a strong observer of **Elizabeth Barrett** herself whose 'novel-poem' **Aurora Leigh** Woolf considered one of the 19th century's most innovative from a women writer. The second, and much-quoted at modern weddings, is to Robert Browning, produced during their secret courtship (for fear of her father's disapproval), and then marriage.

How do I love thee? (Sonnet 43)

How do I love thee? Let me count the ways.
I love thee to the depth and breadth and height
My soul can reach, when feeling out of sight
For the ends of Being and ideal Grace.
I love thee to the level of every day's
Most quiet need, by sun and candlelight.
I love thee freely, as men strive for Right;
I love thee purely, as they turn from Praise.
I love with a passion put to use
In my old griefs, and with my childhood's faith.
I love thee with a love I seemed to lose
With my lost saints, -- I love thee with the breath,
Smiles, tears, of all my life! -- and, if God choose,
I shall but love thee better after death.

BARRETT
BROWNING

Looking towards
High Peak in spring.
From Mutter's Moor
above Sidmouth.

The Sea Side Walk

We walked beside the sea,
After a day which perished silently
Of its own glory --- like the Princess weird
Who, combating the Genius, scorched and seared,
Uttered with burning breath, 'Ho! victory!'
And sank adown, an heap of ashes pale;
So runs the Arab tale.

The sky above us showed
An universal and unmoving cloud,
On which, the cliffs permitted us to see
Only the outline of their majesty,
As master-minds, when gazed at by the crowd!
And, shining with a gloom, the water grey
Swang in its moon-taught way.

Nor moon nor stars were out.
They did not dare to tread so soon about,
Though trembling, in the footsteps of the sun.
The light was neither night's nor day's, but one
Which, life-like, had a beauty in its doubt;
And Silence's impassioned breathings round
Seemed wandering into sound.

O solemn-beating heart
Of nature! I have knowledge that thou art
Bound unto man's by cords he cannot sever -
And, what time they are slackened by him ever,
So to attest his own supernal part,
Still runneth thy vibration fast and strong,
The slackened cord along.

For though we never spoke
Of the grey water and the shaded rock, -
Dark wave and stone, unconsciously, were fused
Into the plaintive speaking that we used,
Of absent friends and memories unforsook;
And, had we seen each other's face, we had
Seen haply, each was sad.

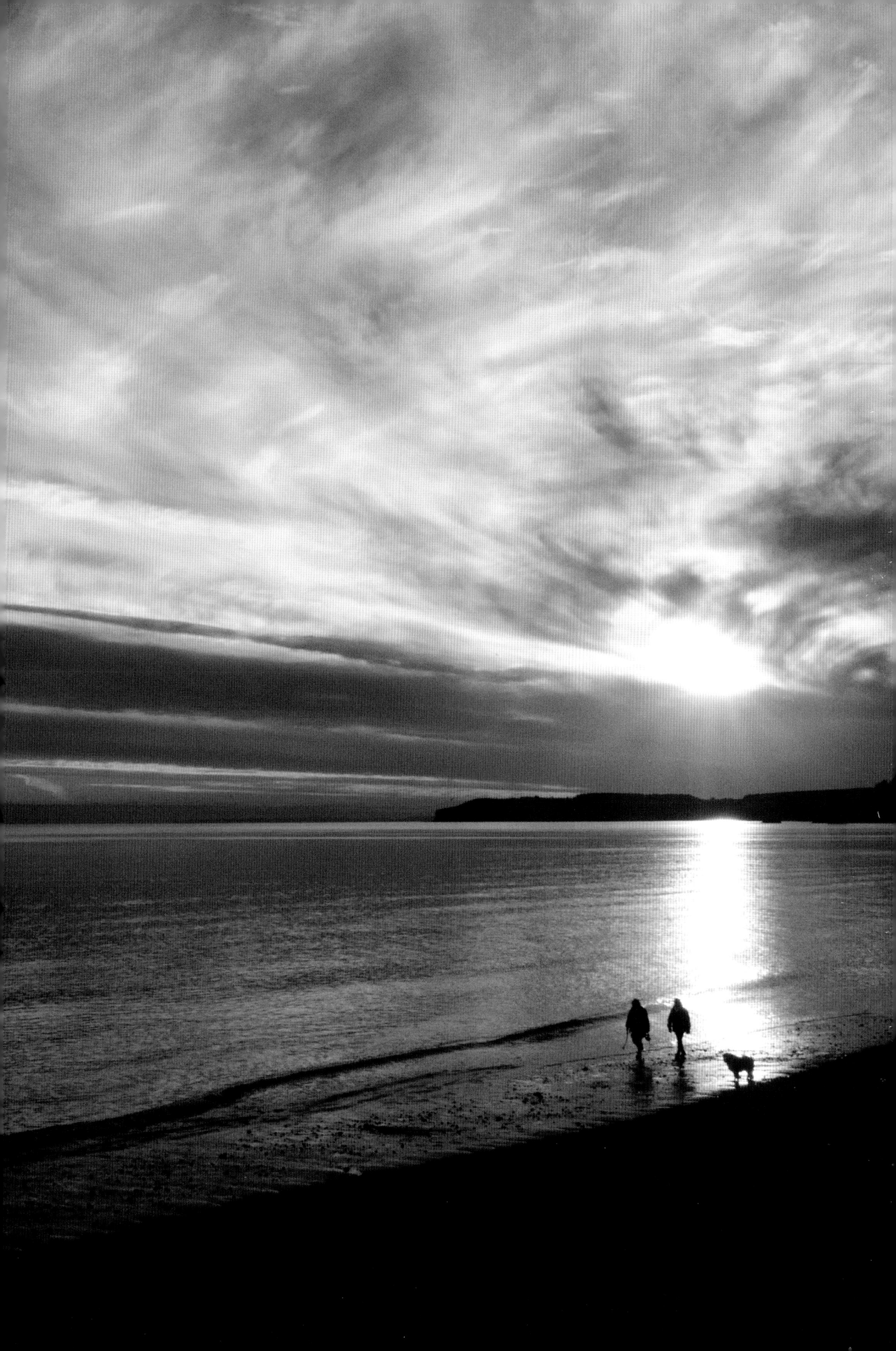

PREVIOUS PAGE
A walk along the
narrowing strip of
sand at Jacob's
Ladder beach, as
the tide advances.

Walk 6 - Elizabeth Barrett 'Sea Side Walk'

It is probable that Elizabeth Barrett's *Sea Side Walk* simply took place along the length of Sidmouth's Esplanade. In the 1830s the extended walkway around to Jacob's Ladder wasn't built. However at low tide she could also have made her way round the headland on the exposed sand at Chit Rocks as today, then continued the full length of the beach as depicted in the photograph on the page above. One assumes she returned the way she came. Remember that the tide only gives about three hours of exposed, walkable sand at Jacob's Ladder before forcing walkers up onto the less amenable shingle stones.

Walk 7 - Salcombe Hill

The cliff walks at Sidmouth are very obvious – essentially 'up' from either end of the sea front. The more recent, owing to the need to cross the river Sid by bridge, climbs Salcombe Hill on the Esplanade's eastern end. It starts at the Alma bridge, then continues up along Cliff Road onto the South West Coastal Path. After passing through an open field the path enters the bluebell wood just below the top (see photo page 58). The view from the summit is superb (see photograph opposite). One can continue eastwards as far as time allows. The path then descends towards Salcombe beach, followed by another up on towards Weston. If time is no object the Coastal Path can be followed all the way to Branscombe (effectively Walk 4 in reverse). But Branscombe and back is a whole day. As to Elizabeth Barrett's 'one dear seat' that 'hangs' over the sea – see the next walk. There are however several remote contenders set in key positions along the way. The bench photographed below is about a mile west of Branscombe.

One of the many
contenders for
**Elizabeth Barrett
Browning's** '*one
dear seat.*' This
one is found about
mid-way between
Branscombe and
Sidmouth.

Walk 8 - Elizabeth Barrett's 'One Dear Seat'

This walk climbs Peak Hill at the western end of the Esplanade. The open field above the beach at Jacob's Ladder now contains a number of newish seats near the top, but none particularly 'lonely.' The Otter sandstone cliffs have eroded and the path changed considerably since 1834, so it is very likely that Elizabeth Barrett's actual seat is gone. However one contender that certainly breathes 'solitude' does exist about a mile further on for those willing to climb up through the woods to the top of Peak Hill (passing beside 'the Gazebo,' Ron Delderfield's perilous cliff-side house during a brief road section). To find it, once on the top of Peak Hill continue along the Coastal Path at first down, then across the open fields to the entrance of the wood under High Peak (see photo on page 77). The solitary bench is encountered just inside the trees at the cliff edge, before the path turns briefly inland. This seat is certainly lonely and does appear to hang over the sea (see photo on page 73). The superb view of the Jurassic coast spreading away into the distance might well inspire a verse. It also may well have inspired H.G. Wells who almost certainly walked this way while thinking up the plot for his short story *The Sea Raiders* (see page 67).

Walk 9 - Along the top of Salcombe Hill

For a very short, easy, flat walk but with a breath-taking view, drive up to the carpark on top of Salcombe Hill then simply walk towards the sea and the cliff edge - about three hundred yards. The way follows the path seen in the photo directly above.

Path along
the summit of
Salcombe Hill

For a fuller picture, literally, of Sidmouth everyday life and that of its environs as encountered by **Elizabeth Barrett,** a good recourse is the work of **Orlando Hutchinson**. (1810-97). This local artist, archaeologist and diarist, lived in Sidmouth all his adult life. A blue plaque can be seen on his house wall in Coburg Terrace, adjoining the bowling green. His diaries are crammed with details of the daily life of a Victorian artist/archaeologist and were recently combined with many of his water-colours in a generous album published by Devon Books, titled **Travels in Victorian Devon,** 1846-1870 (edited by Jeremy Butler).

In it he registers his concerns about the cholera in London sneaking down to Exeter in 1848-49, and reports (and paints) the overturning of his mail coach from Exeter in 1850. We read that a train from Exeter to Paddington in 1851 took twelve hours instead of the promised eight. He complains about an overloaded mail coach in 1852 *'eighteen outside and four in from Ottery to Sidmouth'* in the same year that Sidmouth joined Greenwich Mean Time (until then it was twelve minutes behind). But most striking of all are his paintings of the local landscape, archaeology, incidents and particularly several vivid shipwrecks, see opposite.

However it must be said, not everyone loved Sidmouth. In 1799 the poet **Robert Southey** (1774-1843) visited the town while on one of his walking tours with Coleridge. He described it thus, *'Sidmouth, a nasty watering place infested by lounging ladies and full of footmen.'* But he didn't like Exeter either *'the filthiest place in England,'* or Devon in general – preferring Nether Stowey and Somerset. Southey would later become Poet Laureate (1813-43) and find himself famously reviled by Lord Byron, particularly in his opening Dedication to his poem *Don Juan,* which mentions him by name.

Inclement weather in Sidbury, of the kind not enjoyed by walkers such as Robert Southey.

The schooner "Clementina" driven on shore at Sidmouth, April 1861. She was afterwards unrigged, righted, and floated off.

The war poet **Rupert Brooke** (1887-1915) also made a long enough visit to the town in April 1909 to complete his Sonnet ***'Oh death will find me long before I tire.'*** His parents were staying at Gloucester House on the Esplanade – now The Royal York and Faulkner Hotel. In a letter (to Eddie Marsh) he speaks of *'a long period of fantastic roaming'* in the area and returning from it bare-footed. In a subsequent letter (to Hugh Dalton) he says, referring to the sense of discovering second childhood in Sidmouth, *'I play a great deal on the beach. On reluctant and naked feet I turned from the violet wilderness to the sad breast of my family in their present seaside resort.'*

From this it isn't difficult to picture the twenty-two-year-old poet walking along the sand probably at Jacob's Ladder at low tide, possibly shoes in hand, covering the full mile to the end. There one encounters perfectly smooth yellow sand, silver rock pools draped with green and magenta seaweed, strange waterfalls emerging out of the flesh-like rock. To the right, gigantic red cliffs bear down like the haunches of a huge animal; to the left a hostile tide usually advances. In evening light the colours blend with the deep blue of the sky to indeed make it into a *'violet wilderness.'* Such a place might well have stirred the young poet toward the verses below:

Watercolour made by **Orlando Hutchinson** in 1861. Note the caption made by the artist.

BROOKE

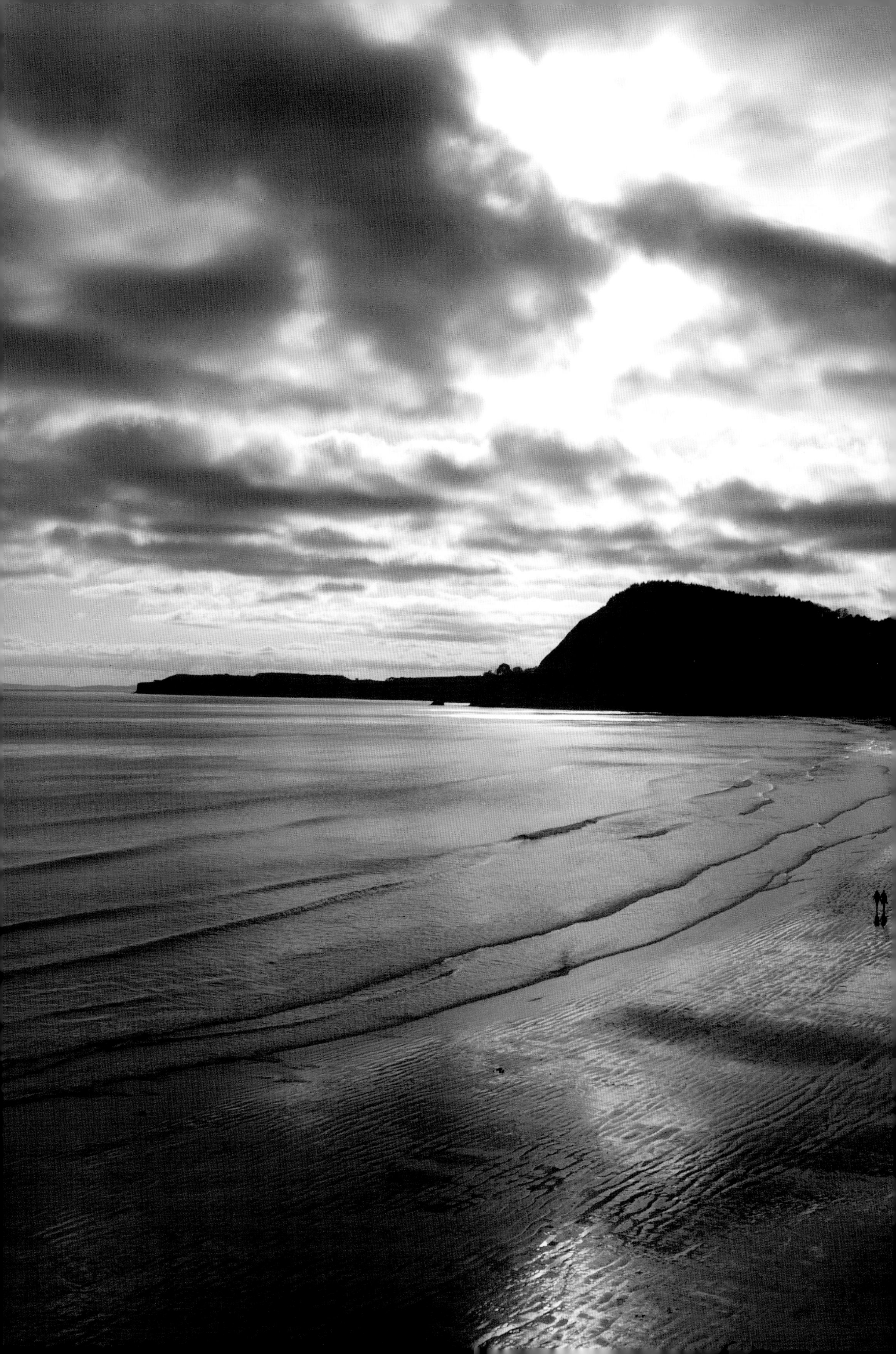

Sonnet

Oh! Death will find me, long before I tire
   Of watching you; and swing me suddenly
Into the shade and loneliness and mire
   Of the last land! There, waiting patiently,

One day, I think, I'll feel a cool wind blowing,
   See a slow light across the Stygian tide,
And hear the Dead about me stir, unknowing,
   And tremble. And I shall know that you have died.

And watch you, a broad-browed and smiling dream,
   Pass, light as ever, through the lightless host,
Quietly ponder, start, and sway, and gleam---
   Most individual and bewildering ghost!

And turn, and toss your brown delightful head
Amusedly, among the ancient Dead.

Some of the above lines were almost
certainly written while walking down this
beach, or as he describes it, *'a violet
wilderness.'* The colour is achieved in
the evening when the red of the Otter
sandstone and beach sand mingles with
the blue of the sky.

85

The end of Fortfield Terrace; cricket pitch in the foreground. The white house on the far right served as **Elizabeth Barrett Browning**'s first Sidmouth home. The new block of flats two buildings to the left, recently replaced the burnt Fortfield Hotel. It has been named *Sanditon* by the developers. See references to **Jane Austen**'s book of the same name, in the adjoining paragraphs.

BERNARD SHAW

AUSTEN

George Bernard Shaw (1856-1950) was also captivated by the atmosphere of Sidmouth. He visited the town's Victoria Hotel in April 1937 during a probable period of exhaustion, although it was later treated as pernicious anaemia and blamed on his vegetarianism. He stayed for several weeks and seemed to recover. On his departure he vowed to return, which he did later. But during his initial stay, frightened of being gawped at or accosted in the hotel's lobby, he chose several times to leave via the fire-escape. The sight of this tall, white-bearded figure climbing down to the ground past their hotel windows, alarmed some of the more sedate guests. This story is related by another East Devon resident **St John Irvine,** in his biography, ***Bernard Shaw, his Life, Work and Friends*** (1956). As friend of Shaw for forty years who lived at Seaton, he seemed to have helped the playwright meet a number of Devon's literati. One such was **Eden Phillpotts** who clearly encountered Shaw in Sidmouth and describes the playwright feeding gulls on the sea front, in his memoir ***From the Angle of 88*** (1951)

Writers often disguise their towns as they do their people, for fear of upsetting the real inhabitants, even if the places they disguise are not one location but a composite. **Jane Austen's** (1775-1817) final but unfinished novel ***Sanditon*** tells the story of a small seaside resort being promoted for all its worth into something it isn't. Often it is thought to be Sidmouth, although there is no conclusive proof. Other towns, like Bexhill and Lyme Regis are also mooted.

While the likelihood is for a composite, the case for Sidmouth is worth noting. Supporters point to similarities between Sidmouth's great developer/investor Emanuel Lousada, who built the town's first cottage orné, 'Sea View' (now rebuilt as 'Peak House') in 1795, and the novel's over-enthusiastic main character

Mr Parker. Both were in the business of promoting the new fashion for taking the waters as it gravitated away from spas like Bath (which **Jane Austen** had never liked) to the new sea-bathing resorts on the English Channel. At the time doctors were prescribing the coastal waters as a cure-all for ailments ranging from deafness to consumption and recommending the winter months with a prior ingestion of a quart of sea-water. As a result, formerly unnoticed fishing villages suddenly found themselves recipients of substantial investment. Many swelled dramatically, their beaches speckled with bathing machines, their fronts dressed with promenades and hotels. Once the resort received a royal visit it was made. Sidmouth was blessed with both George III and Queen Victoria. Architecturally Mr Parker favoured the cottage orné (Sidmouth still has one of the country's best collections) and remarked on **Sanditon's** ripeness for a handsome marine crescent offering superb sea views. This could well be today's Fortfield Terrace.

But whatever the truth, **Jane Austen** did spend the summer of 1801 in Sidmouth with her sister and parents. The trip is made famous by a letter written by her niece Caroline sometime after the author's death, mentioning that Jane met and fell in love with a man on that Devonshire trip who subsequently died. The fact of a mysterious three year gap in **Jane Austen's** correspondence at exactly that period is offered as possible proof that her sister Cassandra destroyed them to maintain the author's secret. But whether one of the world's most 'sensible' writers about love fell victim to the same condition herself in Sidmouth, remains wholly unproven. The story of its irresistible speculation is taken up by a modern author **Jane Gardam** (1928-), whose story **The Sidmouth Letters (**1980) is based on a fictional discovery of the famously lost correspondence and their exploitation.

Clifton Cottage, built in 1820 by Emanuel Lousada as the summerhouse for what is now Peak House. See print from that period on page 75.

'All must linger and gaze on a first return to the sea.'

Jane Austen in *Persuasion*

Elaborate, foliate
bargeboards decorat-
ing the gables of the
Woodlands Hotel on
Station Road. The
former building on
this site was owned
by Sir Walter Raleigh.

Another disguising of Sidmouth that may be less disputed is **William Trevor**'s (1928-) novel ***Children of Dynmouth*** (1976). Although its opening sentence declares this fictional town to be *nestled on the Dorset coast*, subsequent detailed description of the unspoilt seaside resort leaves the source of his inspiration pretty clear. Dynmouth's vital statistics are uncannily similar to Sidmouth's. A former fishing town, still relatively small, but after the 18th century *developed prettily as a watering place* with a *belt of shingle that gave way to sand… the town had expanded inland along the valley of the Dyn. At the eastern end of the promenade near the car-parks and the public lavatories there was a fish-packing station… There were three banks in Dynmouth, Lloyds, Barclays and National Westminster… and the ancient Essoldo Cinema in flaking pink, dim and cavernous within. Spreading inland from the cliffs, a golf course had been laid out.*

All the above could apply to Sidmouth in the 1970s. Furthermore Dynmouth's grand Queen Victoria Hotel even matches Sidmouth's own Victoria Hotel by name. But perhaps conclusive proof was delivered in 1986 when the BBC came to make the film of the book. They hired **William Trevor** as script writer - Trevor himself is a long time Devon resident - and not surprisingly chose Sidmouth for the setting.

While the book had sold well and won the prestigious Whitbread Award (1976), the film lacked the power or penetration of the writing and was not received well in the real Dynmouth. The local paper, *The Sidmouth Herald* was inundated with complaining letters after the 1987 broadcast.

But of course, as with all works of literature, the setting must stand second to the ideas and observations presented. Trevor, like many authors attracted to Sidmouth, looked at its picturesque facades, thatched roofs, rose-painted cottage orné windows and felt an urge to cast his eye into its less picturesque shadows. For this he created his 15 year-old anti-hero, Timothy Gedge, a neglected, but strangely savant blackmailer who gets his kicks spying on the town's secret life. As one of the characters put it:

> …*if you looked at Dynmouth one way you saw it prettily, with its teashops and lace; and if you looked at it another way there was Timothy Gedge…*

Timothy, a fatherless, troubled, bored student at Dynmouth Comprehensive, feels rejected by his mother and loathes all forms of what he sees as double-standard. The only creed he follows was delivered by a pot-smoking temporary teacher at the Comprehensive who declared:

> *the souls of the adult people have shrivelled away: they are like last year's rhubarb walking the streets. Only the void is left.*

To compensate, Timothy sees himself as a great hidden talent that must inevitably be unleashed on the world, preferably by Hughie Green of the 1960/70s talent show, *Opportunity Knocks*. To launch his career he puts his name down for Dynmouth's *Spot the Talent* show at the Easter Fête. But his play requires elaborate props. So indulging his latent desire for revenge, he chooses blackmail as the procurement method. He proceeds to threaten various townspeople

Lodge Cottage on Cotmaton Road. For a print of the house shortly after it was built, see page 74.

The Belmont Hotel facing the sea-front, with its grand Victorian gothic entrance.

TREVOR

with exposure of their secret affairs, concealed homosexuality, family tragedies, unless they come up with the goods.

It is easy to picture the author walking around Sidmouth looking in the windows like his character Timothy, imagining the secrets contained behind the closed curtains and locked doors. As writers usually prefer to describe places they know, it is Sidmouth's curtains that are here flung wide. But in the process of painful, and not always accurate revelation by Timothy, **William Trevor** also shows very clearly how human emotion projects onto, and changes the tone of everything around it. And this includes the landscape itself, strongly coloured by the feeling of its inhabitants.

She had loved watching the sea. She'd loved walking by it. She'd loved the stones it smoothed, and its wildness when it flung itself over the promenade wall, scattering gravel and driftwood. Like anger she said.

On the next page a photograph shows the landscape projecting the same emotion back at the town.

For a taste of the home life of some of the last Sidmouthians who made their living out on that wild sea, there is ***Poor Man's House*** (1908) by **Stephen Reynolds** (1881-1919). Set diary-style in the town of Seacombe (yet another fictionalised name for Sidmouth) it gives a vivid if chaotic portrait of a fisherman's

TREVOR

Anger in the sea at Jacob's Ladder, Sidmouth on Valentine's Day 2014.

life, interposed with a rich Devon burr and some photographs of Sidmouth from 1908, for some reason captioned as Seacombe.

Thomas Hardy (1840-1928) is another west country writer with a strong feeling for landscape and its influence on our personality. He resurrected the ancient term 'Wessex' for his novels, with an elaborate cast of geographic characters, some real, some slightly renamed. But the centre remains Dorset, particularly his town of Casterbridge (in fact Dorchester). While his Wessex also extends into north Cornwall (where he met his wife Emma), one might have expected more of East Devon due to its neighbourly status. But a closer look does reveal one brief foray in his novella *The Romantic Adventures of a Milkmaid* (1883), although the main events are set in Silverthorn (actually Silverton, a village in the Exe valley, half a mile beyond the East Devon boundary). However at one point the milkmaid, Margery, is lured away from her hearth and home by the debonair Baron Von Xanten, to the coastal town of 'Idmouth' where his yacht is moored. For this one must certainly read (S)idmouth. In the landscape of her affections the Baron, a combination of Wicked Wolf, Prince Charming and aristocratic benefactor, is set up against Jim Hayward, a local lime-kiln worker.

In the final scene the Baron picks Margery up in his carriage, saying he will take her back to her husband Jim in Silverthorn. But she seems unsure and while she sleeps, the Baron suddenly changes his mind;

HARDY

94

They soon approached the coast near Idmouth. The carriage stopped. Margery awoke from her reverie.

'Where are we?' she said, looking out of the window, with a start. Before her was an inlet of the sea, and in the middle of the inlet rode a yacht, its masts repeating as if from memory the rocking they had practised in their native forest.

'At a little sea-side nook, where my yacht lies at anchor,' he said tentatively. 'Now, Margery, in five minutes we can be aboard, and in half an hour we can be sailing away all the world over. Will you come?'

In the published ending she doesn't, but Hardy a year before his death, noted in the margin of an edition that contained the novella, *A Changed Man* (originally published 1913):

The foregoing finish of the Milkmaid's Adventures by a re-union with her husband was adopted to suit the requirements of the summer number of a periodical in which the story was first printed. But it is well to inform readers that the ending originally sketched was a different one, Margery, instead of returning to Jim, disappearing with the Baron in his yacht at Idmouth after his final proposal to her and being no more heard of in England.

If so, the last line of the story might have been different; quite possibly akin to the one provided a few pages earlier in the published story. It presents the image of that common sight in the 19th century, a departure by sail from the Sidmouth coast:

...the yacht quivered, spread her woven wings to the air, and moved away. Soon she was but a small, shapeless phantom upon the wide breast of the sea.

Calm in the sea and sky at Sidmouth's cricket pitch, summer 2014. For information on literary players, see the next page.

CONAN DOYLE

As a footnote it should be mentioned that Sidmouth's famous sea-front cricket pitch has attracted more than a few authors, and not only as spectators. **Arthur Conan Doyle** (see Chapter 3), was known as an accomplished batsman and bowler. He played here several times, including twice for the Marylebone Cricket Club (MCC) against the Sidmouth Cricket Club. Doyle, a useful all-rounder, played in ten first-class matches for the MCC. His greatest achievement as a bowler was to dismiss the legendary W.G. Grace. Encouraged by his successes he even formed his own team, The Authors who could muster an eleven with a batting-order that might include P.G. Wodehouse, A.A. Milne, J.M. Barrie, Rudyard Kipling, H.G. Wells, or Jerome K. Jerome. It is not known how many of these authors came to Sidmouth for the cricket, but the Devon writer **Eden Phillpotts** (see Chapter 14) is also recorded playing for The Authors.

As for their skill on the pitch, The Authors were often found to be wanting in talent, but it was said, compensated for their low scores with the gravity of their thoughts. In 1902 and 1903 Conan Doyle captained the MCC team that played against the Sidmouth Cricket Club. While Sidmouth won the first match, they could only draw the second.

As for the Devonshire club itself, Sidmouth Cricket Club was founded in 1823 and still has one of the earliest and best coastal pitches in the country (see photograph on page 95). It served as the origin of the Somerset County Cricket Club, who played their first match there. It thrives to this day.

The Authors vs The Artists cricket teams. Match photo, May 1903. **Arthur Conan Doyle** is top centre.

E.W. Hornung   E.V. Lucas   P.G. Wodehouse   J.C. Snaith   G Chowne   Sir A. Conan Doyle   Hesketh Prichard   L.D. Luard   C.M.Q. Orchardson   L.C. Nightingale   A Kinross

C. Gascoyne   Shaun F. Bullock   G. Hillyard Swinstead   Reginald Blomfield   Hon. W.J. James A.E.W. Mason   E.A. Abbey   A. Chevallier Tyler   J.M. Barrie   G.C. Ives   G. Spencer Watson

It was in the dramatic cottage orné above that the writer **Ron Delderfield** wrote his trilogy *The Horseman Riding By.* The third part, *The Green Gauntlet* is set in a disguised East Devon which seems to face similar development threats as today. Fortunately, then it was saved by the fictional campaigner Paul Craddock, who *'If he had never set foot in the place... the whole strip of coast would be sown with red and white dolls' houses and nothing would be growing there except a few front-garden roses and a few back-garden vegetables. Some of the farms, like High Combe and Low Combe, would have long disappeared and in their place would be caravan parks...'* It carries a sober ring of truth for the time of writing (1960s). He renamed Woodbury Common as Blackberry Moor, also under threat. In real life Woodbury was saved and partly, one hopes, with the aid of literature.

Peak Hill cliff with **Ron Delderfield**'s house The Gazebo, perched on its edge. For more details see Chapter 13.

11 The OTTER VALLEY

The Otter valley is a wide green line that runs straight through East Devon, splitting it virtually in half. Beginning in the Blackdown Hills, it and the River Otter wind their way steadily down to the sea at Budleigh Salterton twenty miles away. About two thirds of way along it meets the town of Ottery St Mary where Coleridge sat on its banks as a boy in the 1780s (see page 12). It is also widely believed that Harry Potter did the same owing to the presence of Ottery St Catchpole in several of the Potter books, but especially **Harry Potter and the Goblet of Fire** (2000) and **Harry Potter and the Deathly Hallows,** (2007). Advocates point to the fact that Harry's creator, **J.K. Rowling** (1965 -) studied French and Classics at nearby Exeter University, so must have visited the town – especially for the famous Tar Barrels and witch-burningesque bonfire on the 5th November. Harry Potter's world is unusual in the fantasy genre, as

it exists not as an alternative world (as in say *Lord of the Rings* by J.R.R. Tolkien) but a parallel one. Many of the places Harry visits are real and contemporary, both in name and situation (like King's Cross station). However the degree of wizardry still practised in the Otter valley is open to debate, as is the exact whereabouts of 'The Burrows,' the much-visited home of Harry's friend Ron Weasley and his family. Stoatshead Hill could easily be East Hill, which rises steeply up behind Ottery St Mary. Or again this could be just another case of authorial composite, of the kind explained by **Beatrix Potter** in her portrayal of Sidmouth as Stymouth (see page 56).

Perhaps the writer most enduringly associated with the Otter valley is the poet **Patricia Beer** (1919-99). Born in Exmouth, she died, eighty years later not far away in Upottery, just north of Honiton. She lived most of her life between these two places, save for the inevitable quick look at the outside world, necessary to all writers. But most of her best work is set in the region, and seems to follow an elegant curve starting in the Exe estuary, up along the coast to the Otter valley then on to the river's source high in the Blackdown Hills. Primarily a poet, her work derives its strength from a close physical contact with nature:

The Otter valley, as seen from the hills just south of Newton Poppleford.

BEER

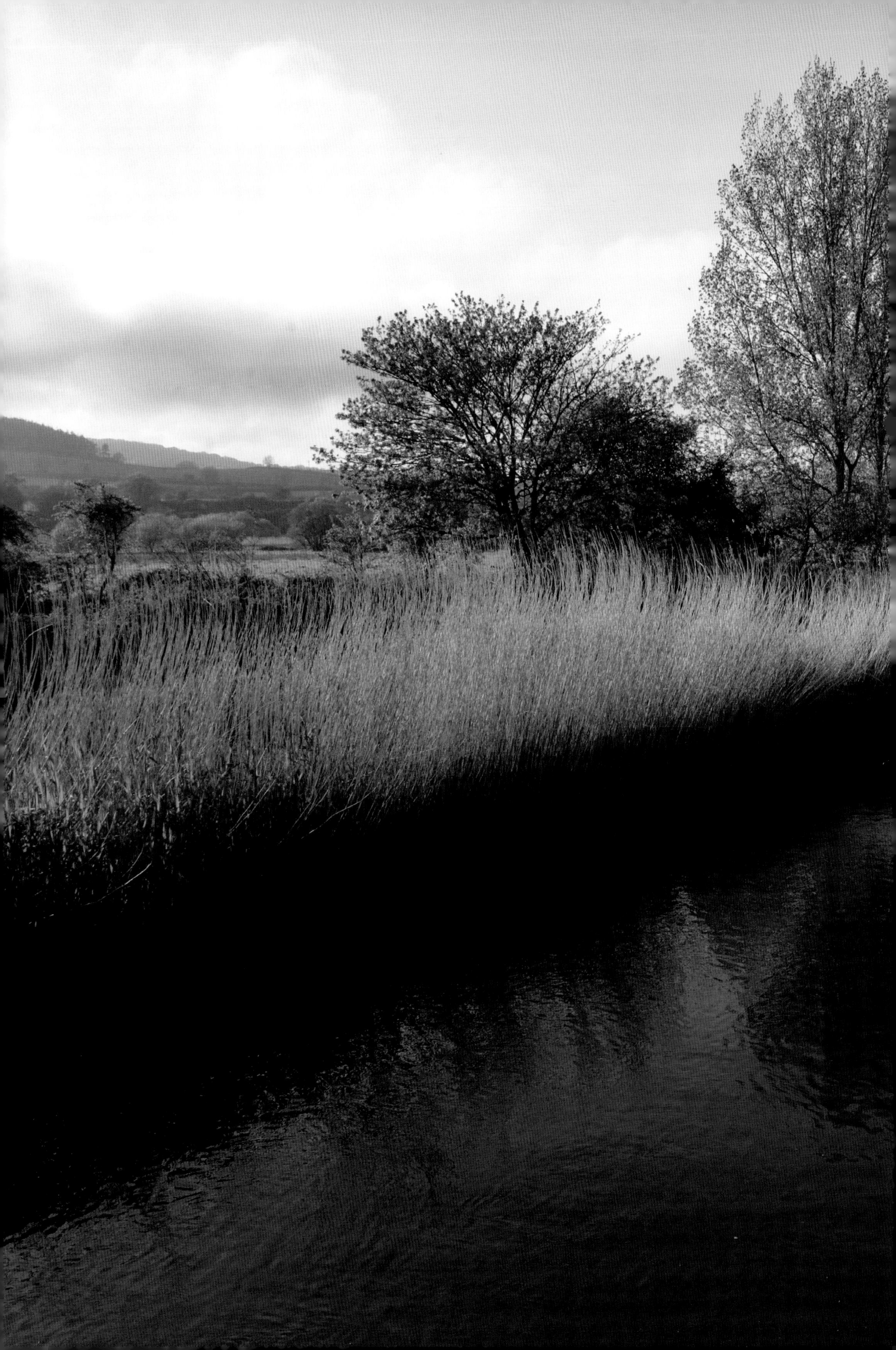

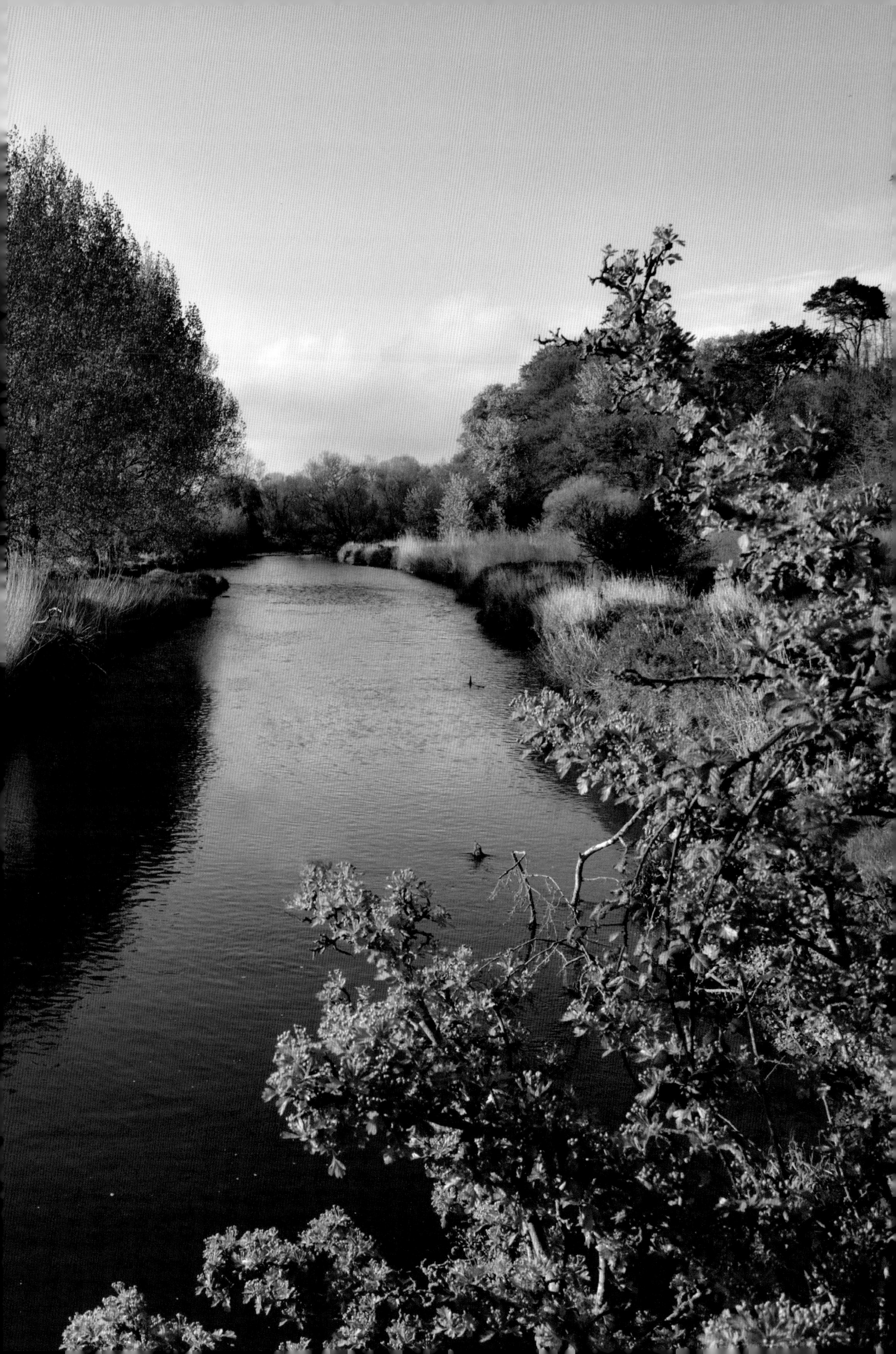

PREVIOUS PAGE
The river Otter near its mouth at Budleigh Salterton. Taken from its last bridge, as described in **Walk 10.** See page 115.

Mist in the Otter Valley

This morning in vivid
Sun, as the gulls flew in,
Their bold shadows advanced
And landed on the stone
Some time before they did.

The mist has come uphill
Now, bringing the river
With it. White, hemlock-cold
Rising. I have never
Seen the valley so full.

It is still day. There might
Be some life left. Somewhere
Farmers may be ploughing
In a bubble of clear
Air, a pocket of sight.

And though with their valiant
Shadows stripped off them, though
Hidden from what they kill,
The gulls are there somehow.
Not a beak less brilliant.

In her autobiography, **Mrs Beer's House** (1968) she describes her unusual Exmouth childhood within the evangelical sect of the Plymouth Brethren (named after the venue of their first UK meeting in 1831). Very strictly bought up, she was trained to see the Exmouth and Torquay tourists as simply ripe for conversion, and so strongly anti-Catholic she reports them describing farting as 'to pope.' Meanwhile her training as a writer began in the singing of hymns, which she says were the first poems she ever knew.

As a girl growing up in 1930s East Devon, excursions to Exeter were considered the height of excitability, although her walk from Exmouth to Ottery St Mary (eight miles) one November probably topped it. The aim had been to see Ottery's famous flaming tar-barrels, but in the end, owing to the crowds, she only witnessed the huge bonfire – which served its purpose because afterwards she finally '*understood how the martyrs could have been burnt alive.*'

The autobiography shows how a poet's eye slowly develops from observations of the things nearest to her, gradually stretching outward with her

BEER

expanding curiosity. After a period of world travelling, she chose to settle back where she began. Along the way she also provides pictures of East Devon now long gone, like the vanished branch railway line from Exmouth to Sidmouth Junction (see the extract from her poem **The Branch Line** on the next page page) where *'each station had a personality of its own.'* How the station at East Budleigh

was the station for the walk to Hayes Barton, birthplace of Sir Walter Raleigh, and to the coast at Ladram Bay where the Spanish Sailors had been washed up after the Armada (my father used to say that the word Ladram meant 'the grave of Spanish sailors' but I never heard his reasons) and smugglers had hidden contraband in caves. It was also the starting place for the best walk of all; down the banks of the Otter to . [where]… The lavish growth of the meadow trailed over to the water. The river moved quite strongly and long plants with yellow flowers stretched out downstream like horses' tails decorated for the Carnival.

Mist above the Otter Valley, in the trees at Mutter's Moor, near Sidmouth.

BEER

103

Enshrined under this bough is a view of the Otter Valley from just above Otterton. Woodbury Common breaks the skyline. The former rail branch line travelled from Sidmouth Junction (now defunct), down this valley, eventually on to Exmouth, then Exeter.

The Branch Line (extract)

One train was the last,
Decorated with a crowd
Of people who like last things,
Not normally travellers,
Mostly children and their fathers,
It left to a theatrical blast
As the guard for once played
At his job, with mixed feelings…

…The platform is now old
And empty, but still shows
The act of waiting.
Beyond it the meadows,
Where once the toy shadows
Of funnel and smoke bowled,
Are pure green, and no echoes
Squeeze into the cutting.

BEER

For a map showing the route of this line, see page 130

She then goes on to describe the carnival itself at Exmouth, with its horse-drawn tableaux; '*The Littleham contingent was particularly good. They sent in at least six 'tablows' which were usually poetic and pretty, rather than satirical and humorous as the Exmouth ones tended to be. A typical Exmouth entry was 'Rent in Arrears'* with a woman spanking her son. Later she wrote one novel, a historical portrait of the Otter valley region, called ***Moon's Ottery*** (1979).

Set around the time of the Spanish Armada, the intention of this slightly eccentric novel was clearly to provide the everyday landscape with the characters that made it what it is today. Included is Rolle (a local land-owner based on Lord Rolle whose family developed Exmouth's dock area); Mutter (a local farmer), with its link to Mutter's Moor near Sidmouth; and Suckbitch, an unflattering re-spelling of the local Saxon name Sokespitch - see ***Travels in Georgian Devon*** by the **Reverend John Swete** (1752-1821), volume IV page 172, edited by Todd Gray. She also includes a white witch (in 1587 witches were often preferred to doctors), and the ever-present fear of cholera and Spanish invasion by sea. By attaching the drama to local landmarks - the Armada even makes a brief entry sailing in formation past the cliffs of Sidmouth and Branscombe – the origins of names like the Beacon in Exmouth become all the more vivid. The strong presence of farm animals, fields, landed gentry and the eternally glinting sea with its merchant ships sailing up the Exe to the Exeter docks, illustrates the key to the wealth of the region, aided by its then flourishing wool trade.

The Spanish Armada being defeated by Sir Francis Drake (another Devonian), with some help from the weather. Painted by an unknown, 16th century English artist.

12 BUDLEIGH SALTERTON

RALEIGH

In 1870 the Pre-Raphaelite painter John Everett Millais created a picture that would become one of his most famous. It shows two boys sitting on the beach at Budleigh Salterton three hundred years ago, at a key moment in British history. Beside them lies a model of what at the time represented the height of modern technology, a fully-sailed galleon. Their eyes are fixed in rapt attention on a Genoese sailor whose right hand gestures dramatically out to sea. The boys are **Walter Raleigh** (1552–1618) and his brother Carew who grew up a couple of miles away at Hayes Barton Farm, East Budleigh. Millais named his painting '*The Boyhood of Raleigh.*'

One reason for the image's popularity is its portrayal of the moment a young boy's thoughts are awakened to what may lie beyond the horizon. But in Raleigh's case the imagination of the child would very untypically become the reality for the man. **Sir Walter Raleigh** has entered history as Britain's prototype Renaissance Man, teenage soldier in France, sea-captain at 26, courtier for Queen Elizabeth 1st, poet whose verses were compared to Shakespeare's (his contemporary), Queen's favourite, explorer, first coloniser of Virginia, prisoner in the Tower of London, founder of the important but secretive 'School of Night,' and also crucially, introducer of the potato to Britain. Some locals still claim Britain's first-ever potato patch as a walled garden near the church at Colaton Raleigh.

For our purpose Millais' picture also vividly demonstrates how a landscape can affect the imagination of those growing up within it. The fact of a Genoese sailor sitting on the beach at Budleigh in the 16th century illustrates how surprisingly cosmopolitan East Devon was. The international space of the sea beyond its cliffs served, and serves still, as a main artery of cultural material flowing from Europe to our island. Indeed some argue it is more important than

RALEIGH

The 'Boyhood of Raleigh,' painted by John Everett Millais in 1870 while staying at the Octagon, in Budleigh Salterton.

ever, as the land of East Devon and the country beyond can no longer support its own population. We are all in the hands of the ships that miraculously keep appearing on that wide channel of water beyond the Budleigh coast.

In those days it was sailed not only by local fishermen and transportation ships (then it was usually quicker to travel to London by sea than land), but also haunted by French pirates, threatened by Spanish invaders, traversed by Dutch, German, Flemish merchants, some of whom would have wrecked on its shores during storms. The activity out on that watery movie screen wouldn't take long to inspire this Devonshire squire's son to follow that Genoese finger. Thus, in 1569, while still a teenager and a loyal Protestant like his father, he sailed over to France to assist the fleeing Huguenots during their steady defeat by the Catholic army.

But the roots of Walter Raleigh and his family sink deep into the East Devon soil. They can be traced back to the 12th century at least, partly evidenced by the names of nearby villages, Colaton Raleigh and Combe Raleigh. A visit to East Budleigh's All Saints' church still finds the front pew bearing the crest of the Raleigh family, along with some other remarkable 15th and 16th century pew-end carvings, including images of galleons, American Indians, exotic foliage, local and foreign faces, fishes, and patterns of all sorts. Again the cosmopolitan sea influences entering the South West of England (see photos on page 112).

Inevitably Raleigh's strong relationship with the sea finds itself reflected in his poetry, such as the verse below from his poem **The Ocean to Cynthia**, dedicated to Queen Elizabeth (who called him 'Water');

To seek new worlds, for gold, for praise, for glory
To try desire, to try love severed far
When I was gone she sent her memory
More stronger than were ten thousand ships of war
To call me back

RALEIGH

Clearly impressed by the wit and intelligence of her gallant courtier, known for throwing his coat into a puddle before her, Elizabeth soon promoted him to Lord Lieutenant of Cornwall and Vice Admiral of the West, keeping him close to her at court for ten years. Raleigh was tall and flamboyant, proud of his Devon accent, which the Queen liked to mimic. In 1584 he was elected a Member of Parliament for Devon and even after Elizabeth imprisoned him in the tower for his secret marriage to one of her Maids of Honour, she soon released him to sort out a potential rebellion in Dartmouth, caused by the arrival of a captured Portuguese treasure ship. He achieved his task having been cheered by the locals on his arrival into the town.

However his flamboyant and passionate nature inevitably inspired enemies. This Renaissance Man was imprisoned several times for duelling. He also wrote one of the most audacious poems in English literature for its day, *The Lie* (c.1592), the spirit of which was probably responsible for his head ending

Statue of **Sir Walter Raleigh** found in East Budleigh, close to the church.

Hayes Barton Farm set on the slopes rising above East Budleigh. Birthplace of **Sir Walter Raleigh.**

up in a basket in 1618. On its publication his enemies eagerly accused him of atheism (then punishable by death) and he was banished from court, although still retaining Queen Elizabeth's favour. Below are the two opening verses:

Go, Soul, the body's guest,
Upon a thankless errand;
Fear not to touch the best;
The truth shall be thy warrant:
Go, since I needs must die
And give the world the lie

Say to the Court it glows
And shines like rotten wood
Say to the Church it shows
What's good and doth no good
If Church and Court reply,
Then give them both the lie

RALEIGH

But it was the application of the young Raleigh's imagination from that moment on the East Devon beach, which created the man. His later-named *'School of Night,'* was a secretive but influential group of thinkers, artists, scientists and nobility. Their associates included Thomas Harriot (1560-1621, the astronomer and mathematician); Christopher Marlowe (1564-1593, author of the play *'Dr Faustus'*); John Dee (1527-1609, the alchemist, Hermetic philosopher and mathematician); and George Chapman (1559-1634, dramatist and poet). They would meet away from the prying eyes of the Church to discuss the most advanced ideas of the day. Dubbed 'The School of Atheism' by certain clerics and enemies, it nevertheless helped some of the forward-most thinkers apply their discoveries. As an admiral, Raleigh insisted that all sea captains learn the most advanced navigation techniques. Partly as a result the English soon became the world's best seamen. Similarly, the ship designers were encouraged to employ the latest technology, and the Spanish navy found themselves having to copy the English galleon design.

However the enemies to the *'School of Night'* members were formidable and some funded by Raleigh's direct rivals at court, particularly the Earls of Essex and Southampton. While it may be expected for someone of Raleigh's status

RALEIGH

to have their life satirised, when the satirist is William Shakespeare, then the battle is truly on. It has been argued that the character Armado in Shakespeare's *Love's Labour's Lost* (1593-4) is based on Raleigh. Sir Walter was known for his eloquent literary longing, particularly in poetry dedicated to Queen Elizabeth, so Shakespeare had his character Don Armado write a letter to the King (of Spain) saying how desperately he is '*besieged by a sable-coloured melancholy.*'

At the same time Raleigh wrote poems that have been compared to those of Shakespeare. For instance his equivalent to the '*Seven Ages of Man:*'

What is our Life?

What is our Life, the play of passion
Our mirth, the Music of Division
Our Mothers womb, the Tyreing houses be
Where we are drest for lifes short comedy
The Earth the stage Heaven the Spectator is
who sits and views whosoere doth Act amiss
The graves which hide us from the scorching Sun
Are like drawn Curtains till the play is done
Thus playing post we to our latest rest
And then we die in earnest not in Jest.

In these lines are clues as to how he charmed the Queen. At one time, so the story goes, he offered a bet that he could weigh the smoke puffed out of his famous pipe - Raleigh is credited as the first populariser of tobacco smoking in England. She accepted, at which point he weighed the pipe before smoking it, and then afterwards. The difference he said, was the smoke's weight. She paid up, joking that many a man had turned gold into smoke, but very few smoke into gold. His final poem was found transcribed in a copy of the bible, left in the Gatehouse of the Tower of London.

Lines Written on the Eve of his Execution

Even such is Time, which takes in trust
Our youth, our joys, and all we have,
And pays us but with age and dust;
Who in the dark and silent grave,
When we have wandered all our ways,
Shuts up the story of our days:
And from which earth, and grave, and dust,
The Lord shall raise me up, I trust.
(1618)

Pew-end carvings from All Saints' church at East Budleigh. Top left is the front pew bearing the Raleigh coat of arms. Created mostly in the 15th and 16th centuries they show the influences already entering East Devon from the Americas and beyond..

113

MORALL

To bring the beach at Budleigh and its distinctive flat pebbles right up to date, the Exeter-born author **Clare Morrall** (1952-) set her novel *The Man Who Disappeared* (2010) in the town behind it, Budleigh Salterton. This modern-day portrait of a middle-class family thrown into chaos, opens when the father, an accountant, is accused of money-laundering, whereupon he suddenly and mysteriously vanishes. While the police try to hunt him down, the family find their bank accounts frozen, the press camped outside their door, the children harassed at school. Meanwhile the wife Kate struggles to understand how she married such a deceiver. After their elegant Edwardian home on the Budleigh cliff-side is repossessed, their troubles eventually reach a denouement on the mud-flats between Lympstone and Exmouth, as the tide advances. This fantastic open expanse of either land or sea serves as a useful stage-front for any kind of drama, be it depictions of landscape or an attempted murder. However the living, real-life estuary can be viewed more placidly and in full, by taking the **Walk 11** explained on page 125.

TROLLOPE

It seems also that the Trollope family carry some links with Budleigh Salterton. Anthony Trollope met his first biographer there, Thomas Escott. Later his brother **Thomas Adolphus Trollope** (1810-92), also a novelist and travel writer, moved to the house Cliff Corner in 1887. Until then he had been living in Italy and there was very friendly with another East Devon-to-Italy ex-pat, **Elizabeth Barrett Browning** (see page 72). However the original Cliff Corner was demolished in the 1930s, although the replacement still carries a blue plaque.

Contemplative atmosphere on the last day of the Budleigh Literary Festival. Budleigh sea-front, September 2014.

Budleigh Salterton is so named for its former salt works. While these are long gone, the town has more recently been finding a new kind of identity within the literary festival circuit. The **Budleigh Salterton Literary Festival** was started by locals back in 2008 and grown modestly ever since. Although still small it now attracts an impressive line of mainstream writers, thanks partly to its President, the novelist **Hilary Mantel** (1952-) of *Wolf Hall* fame, who is a town resident. The four days of talks are held mostly in Budleigh's churches and civic halls and the event seems to fit neatly within the body of the town. Just as Budleigh's open, unprotected beach-front welcomes visitors to the sea without fanfare, so too an atmosphere of contemplation and philosophy is quietly returning to this discreet corner of East Devon.

Walk 10 - Walter Raleigh East Budleigh and the Otter

For a good walk that could be dubbed 'The Raleigh Way Home,' as it begins on Budleigh beach and leads to East Budleigh, start at the car park at the eastern end of Budleigh Salterton. Follow the Otter valley along the South West Coastal Path for nearly a mile, as far as the bridge over the Otter (where the photograph on page 100 was taken). Don't cross it but continue north along the river bank (western side). The next village appearing on the left hand side is East Budleigh. There is now a choice: either turn up into East Budleigh or continue along the river another mile to Otterton Mill, (now a working mill with its excellent café and bakery). For East Budleigh look out for the two left hand turns away from the river towards the village; the second is better and is found more or less directly opposite the point where the houses begin. To find the village's All Saint's Church with the carved pew ends (see photos on pages 112 and 113), walk up through the village centre towards its highest point. Almost directly opposite is the Walter Raleigh pub. Hayes Barton, Walter Raleigh's birth place, is a further mile and a half along the narrow road that meanders away from the village. It starts directly opposite the pub.

13 EXMOUTH

One of the most dramatically sited cottages ornés in the whole of East Devon, if not England, was built by the Exmouth-bred playwright and author **Ronald Delderfield,** (1912-72). Although not situated in Exmouth but Sidmouth, the 'Gazebo' (see photo on page 97), sitting on the upper flanks of Peak Hill, embodies the full romantic spirit of this Exmouth man. Few houses can be more beautifully or perilously positioned. While this round-walled, thatched cottage offers one of the finest views in Devon, all the way up the Jurassic coast to Portland Bill, the huge airy drop beyond its garden keeps taking new great gulps out of the grass towards it. The speed of this was probably not foreseen by its creator, and today the cottage stands just a few metres from the edge of England. Soon one fears, it may make a

DELDERFIELD

Exmouth estuary as seen from the Beacon. Here the tide is in so the sandbank, normally directly ahead, is invisible. In the foreground stands the Jubilee Clock Tower, built in 1897.

dramatic exit. The same is true for the memorial plaque bearing **R.F. Delderfield's** name, which stands beside the old cliff-road up Peak Hill, right at the point where the tarmac of the abandoned road now hangs out into space.

However the man who built so romantically drew most of his inspiration not from Sidmouth where he eventually died, but seven miles to the west in Exmouth.

The young **Ron Delderfield** arrived at the mouth of the river Exe not long after his eleventh birthday, and sporting a cockney accent. His father had boldly upped sticks in London and purchased the ailing *Exmouth Chronicle* (1882-1962), at the time situated at 3 Chapel Hill (now a restaurant), with the idea of transforming it and his family's fortunes into a going concern. This was to give the young Ron a more than lively adolescence in the burgeoning holiday town of Exmouth, helped considerably by a first job as reporter on his father's paper. From this he would gather the material that later allowed him to write his West End hit ***Worm's Eye View*** (1944) and the play ***The Bull***

Brochure advertising Exmouth beach from around the time that Delderfield worked for the *Chronicle*. The red Orcombe Point cliffs in the background mark the start of East Devon's Jurassic Coast.

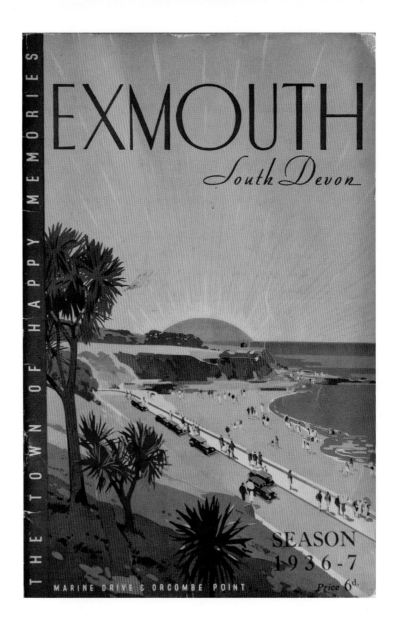

Boys from which the first 'Carry On' film, *Carry On Sergeant* was derived. For a naturally mischievous boy from Bermondsey, the sudden presence of a long sandy beach, sweeping estuary, and miniature but active port, began to prime the literary motor. As he put it in his autobiography **Bird's Eye View** (1954):

> *Exmouth, as a district, provided far more in the way of romantic background than I had dared to hope. In the early twenties it had not yet reached the point of no return that faces every coastal town at some time in its normal development – that of deciding whether it wants to be a Blackpool or a Bournemouth, a Budleigh Salterton or a .*
>
> *It had a small dock, a half-developed marine-drive, two or three streets of old-fashioned shops and a population of 10,000. … a town where the guide book assured them "sea-breezes were tempered with warm south-west winds precluding the possibility of severe winters."*
>
> *The miniature dock was the best playground in town. It was surrounded by timber yards and in its basin one could clamber aboard the very last of*

DELDERFIELD

118

Photograph of **Ron Delderfield** in his 50s.

the coastal sail-driven tramps, low-hulled vessels no bigger than the Golden Hind, with rakish masks, blue and gold cabins and reefer-wrapped skippers who spoke no English whatever and possessed a strange inability to see boys climbing their rigging…

Nor was this all. Four hundred yards across the strait, and separated from the pier by a mill-race tide, was the Warren, a sandy peninsula covered with bungalows that were always being wrecked by gales and therefore provided a plenitude of firewood for the distress beacons we lit when, as shipwrecked mariners, we sought to attract the attention of passing ships…

That Estuary was always like the Mississippi early mornings and late at night… The only thing the setting lacked in the way of a Twain duplicate was a steamboat 'fighting the big water in the middle...

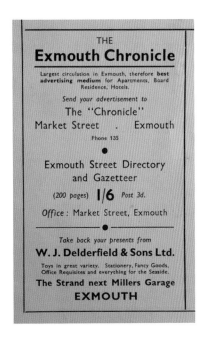

THE
Exmouth Chronicle

Largest circulation in Exmouth, therefore **best advertising medium** for Apartments, Board Residence, Hotels.

Send your advertisement to
The "Chronicle"
Market Street . Exmouth
Phone 135

●

Exmouth Street Directory and Gazetteer
(200 pages) **1/6** Post 3d.

Office: Market Street, Exmouth

●

Take back your presents from
W. J. Delderfield & Sons Ltd.
Toys in great variety. Stationery, Fancy Goods, Office Requisites and everything for the Seaside.
The Strand next Millers Garage
EXMOUTH

An advertisement in the same brochure (opposite) for **Ron Delderfield's** father's two businesses -*The Exmouth Chronicle* and the shop run by his mother.

PREVIOUS PAGE
From this angle
Exmouth's western
sea front looks very
similar to that in
Delderfield's day. In
fact the port just be-
hind the Esplanade
has been complete-
ly redeveloped into
a large apartment
complex, effectively
making the harbour
a marina.

The [Exmouth] promenade terminated in a long buttress of red sandstone cliffs, followed by caverns as good and as gloomy as any in the books. I went down there that first Christmas Day and thought myself the most fortunate lad in the world.

After being painstakingly taught a Devonshire accent and phraseology by his mother's shop assistant – such as 'Where be us gwarn then?' - which translates as 'Where are we going?' (as quoted in his memoire **For My Own Amusement,** 1962), at the age of seventeen his father enlisted him as a full-time reporter on the revamped *Chronicle*. He excelled and became known for his feverish pedalling behind fire engines to be the first on the story. But when not uncovering the newsworthy in Exmouth weekly life he started writing plays, such as **Fleet Street in Lilliput** (1932) about a man struggling to convert a newspaper, The District Post, at a seaside resort called Sandcombe, from a sleepy non-entity to a thriving, contemporary journal. Dramas collected for this and other *Chronicle* articles would later be reworked and appear in the West End as his play **Printer's Devil** - then a film starring Cyril Cusack and Stanley Baxter. His best-received novel **A Horseman Riding By** (1966), is partly set in East Devon. For more details and a photo of the dramatic place he wrote it, see page 97. The novel would be serialised by the BBC in 1978, six years after his death. Another work with strong regional connections is the historical novel **Farewell the Tranquil Mind** (1950) which is set partly around the Littleham area. Delderfield was deeply committed to Devon's landscape and campaigned hard to save Woodbury Common from development. Thanks to him and others like him today it, and nothing else, cuts the region's skyline from most directions. In an article written for *Devon Life* magazine in March 1965 he said:

Looking back I find it odd to see how insistently Devon tugs at the creative impulse, how mercilessly she jogs the elbow and drives a man hopelessly off course.

Sitting up in the Gazebo at Sidmouth, looking at one of the finest views in the county, one can easily see how this might happen. Indeed he rarely cut the hedge directly in front of his study window because otherwise *'I would never write a word.'* He, like most writers, used walking through the landscape to help gather his ideas (**Thomas Hardy** was famous for scribbling phrases on leaves). Often he would be seen among the gorse and ferns of Sidmouth's Mutter's Moor, while knowing all too well that being *'off course'* was in fact his stock-and-trade.

Exmouth also served as a temporary home to the wife of one of literature's most serial philanderers (and geniuses), Lord George Byron. Anne Isabella Milbanke, subsequently **Lady Byron**, came to the Beacon in 1828 already a widower. Although their marriage lasted only a year, she became mother to his only official child, Ada Lovelace, who subsequently worked with the

BYRON

122

mathematician Charles Babbage and is described as the world's first computer programmer. She arrived with her daughter at this small hill facing the English Channel and the Exe estuary. The magnificent view, with receding south Devon coastline before an appearing then disappearing sandbank, also presented the daily sea traffic, including merchant and slave ships sailing up the estuary to the ports of Topsham and Exeter. This may well have helped inspire her strong abolitionist activities. She later became one of the more prominent women in the anti-slavery movement. A more specific account of the movement's activities in and around Exmouth and Exeter can be found in local author **Richard Bradbury's** historical novel ***Riversmeet*** (2007).

Below is the poem ***The Estuary*** by **Patricia Beer** (see page 99) in full, which describes what this view meant to one born and bred in Exmouth:

Looking up at the Beacon from the Esplanade.

BRADBURY

Byron Court, up on the Beacon; formerly The Byron Hotel. Lady Byron's favourite UK location at which to take the sea air.

The Estuary
A light elegant wall waves down
The riverside, for tidiness
Or decoration – this water
Needs little keeping in – but turns
The corner to face the ocean
And thickens to a bastion.

No one can really taste or smell
Where the salt starts but at one point
The first building looks out to sea
And the two sides of the river
Are forced apart by cold light
And wind and different grasses.

I see this now. But at one time
I had to believe that the two
Sides were almost identical.
I was a child who dared not seem
Gloomy. Traversing grey water
From the east side where I was born

And had spent a normal cross life,
To live gratefully with strangers
On the west side, I grinned and clowned.
I did not go back for ages
And became known for cheerfulness
In a house where all was not well.

Grief was a poltergeist that would
Not materialise but broke
Everything. Neither believed in
Nor dreaded, it took one decade
To appear, one to be recognised,
Then cleared the air wonderfully

So that nowadays I am able
To see the estuary as two
Distinct pieces of countryside,
Not a great deal to choose between
Them perhaps but at least different,
Rising normally from two roots.

On one bank stiff fields of corn grow
To the hilltop, are draped over
It surrealistically.
On the other, little white boats
Sag sideways twice every day
As the sea pulls away their prop.

Walk 11 - Ron Delderfield The Exe Estuary

This follows the East Devon Way along the Exe estuary up to Lympstone (or _Redcliff_ - see next chapter). Depending on the state of the tide and weather, the view is either glinting water or the reddish-brown mud of the cockle sands. Because Exmouth port has been redeveloped into houses, this flat, two-mile walk now begins at the far (northern) end of the coach-park linked to Exmouth railway station, through a tiny slot in the hedge right beside the estuary. It follows the water much of the way. The wide open space to the left is also the venue for an attempted murder in the climactic final scene of _The Man Who Disappeared_ by Clare Morrall (see page 114). The return journey can be made either by foot, back along the same path, or by rail from Lympstone railway station back to the terminus at Exmouth.

The elbow of the Exe estuary at low tide. Exmouth harbour is directly behind; Starcross ahead across the water.

125

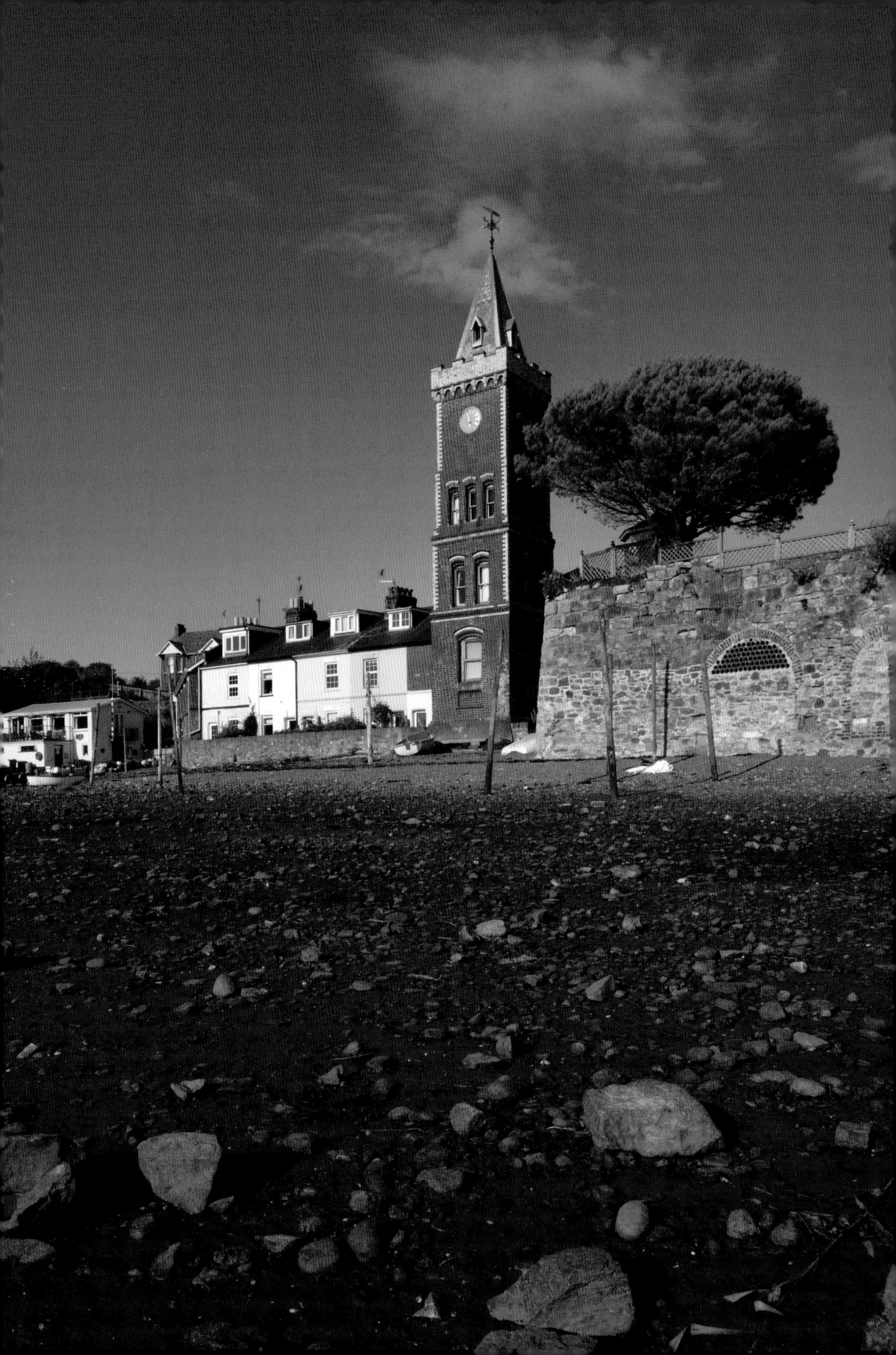

LYMPSTONE

The estuary of Devon's largest river, the Exe, is one of the region's liveliest natural spectacles. Twice a day the tide sucks away the huge expanse of salt water to expose a dozen square miles of rich, reddish-brown mudflats, to the delight of the waders, dippers, curlews and other long-beaked and -legged birds. There is no better place to observe such a grand, pre-historic opera than at the village set at its centre, Lympstone.

Possibly for this reason alone the village was chosen as setting for a novel by one of the region's most prolific, but now strangely forgotten writers, **Eden Phillpotts** (1862-1960). This dedicated Devon man and President of the Dartmoor Preservation Association was at one point in his career a household name. He wrote over 130 novels and 55 plays. Alfred Hitchcock made a film of his West End hit, *A Farmer's Wife* (1928). Many of his 18 Dartmoor novels ended up as bestsellers. Over his long life he would publish 225 major works - a prodigious figure for any writer. On novels alone he averaged nearly two a year during his adult life. It could be argued that if he had written less he might have been more successful - in line with James Joyce's statement about himself, that although capable of writing a novel a year, it was better for the world that he didn't.

PHILLPOTTS

Eden Phillpotts in mid-career. He lived until the age of 98.

OPPOSITE
The centre of Lympstone, identified across the estuary by Peter's Tower built in 1885 (now a Landmark Trust property).

'You never enjoy the world aright, till the Sea itself floweth in your veins,

Thomas Traherne

till you are clothed with the heavens, and crowned with the stars'

(1636-1674)

But what makes Phillpotts particularly interesting is the way he chose his subjects – by landscape. With a few exceptions, most of his best work concerns Devon, to the extent the county becomes a giant character in itself, each book exploring it from a different location, with its own unique characteristics and people. His novel **Redcliff** (1924) – a renamed Lympstone – is tackled in similar epic style, with a Dickensian cast of characters, the landscape itself serving as the lead. Below is the novel's opening paragraph:

> *Upon the broad estuary of the Exe lies Redcliff, and the fishermen's quarters thrust so near its brink that at spring tides, under push of an equinoctial gale, the highways are invaded and ducks swim in the little streets. The houses cluster along the shingle and face west… Within the Cove are sheds and lockers; beyond it rise poles for drying of nets; while round about this snug spot ascend red cliffs, weathered and fretted to beauty, crowned with horrent scrub of elm brushed brusquely back from their foreheads by the western wind.*

He then paints in the internal workings of the village, starting with a conversation held on the platform of Redcliff's railway station, one of the few East Devon branch lines not closed after the first Beeching Report of 1963. Here locals compare their village with the nearby, swelling resort of Exmouth which they describe as:

Map of East Devon railway stations in 1908. The dotted section marks the branch lines lost after the Beeching Report of 1963. The trains were frequently described by the region's writers: such as C. Day Lewis, Patricia Beer (see poem on page 104) and Eden Phillpotts.

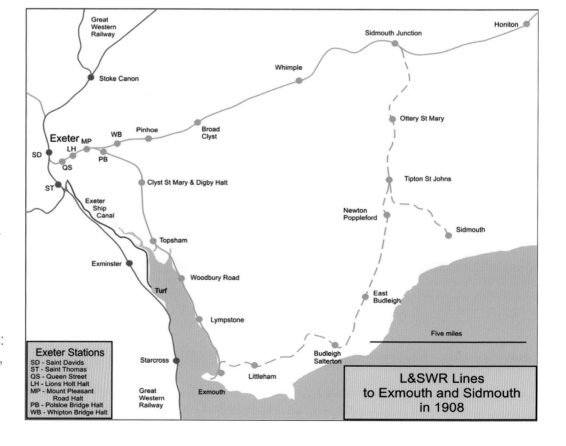

Exeter Stations
SD - Saint Davids
ST - Saint Thomas
QS - Queen Street
LH - Lions Holt Halt
MP - Mount Pleasant Road Halt
PB - Polsloe Bridge Halt
WB - Whipton Bridge Halt

L&SWR Lines to Exmouth and Sidmouth in 1908

130

Church street,
Lympstone.

a place almost sprung up within living knowledge, whereas Redcliff goes back
for hundreds of years… We've got the dignity and they've got the money.

After this his brush extends to the estuary shore where the women
cockle-rakers are going '*down to tide*' in '*the mud-flats spread out in the afternoon*
sunshine [with] their humped backs like stranded whales above a network of shallow
waters.'

The characters of Redcliff, and therefore Lympstone itself, are slowly
uncovered strata by strata, always one feels, subservient to the place they inhabit,
although they don't know it. In Chapter 3 we meet Mrs Denning.

PHILLPOTTS

PHILLPOTTS

*She had a nose like Dante's and lustreless, pallid eyes, which having suffered
from disease in youth, never fully recovered. Her mouth was firm and small,
her countenance long and narrow. Upon her hair she wore a heavy coil of
faded gold. It had grown there in her remote past and been cut off during
her illness. She had preserved it however, and worn it ever since. It was to be
buried with her. People called it 'Miss Denning's halo.'*

Phillpotts is an example of a writer with a strong cause. The county of
Devon itself provided him with his prodigious energy and health; he fell just
short of 100. He spent his childhood in Dawlish, then, after a period in London,
to which he apparently never returned, even to see his most successful West End
plays, he moved to Torquay. For the final 31 years of his life he resided at Kerswell
House, Broadclyst. For details of this last period in East Devon, along with his
many significant literary visitors and associations, such as with Agatha Christie,
see page 144.

When not engaged in somewhat convoluted conversations (the book's
432 pages are mostly speech) he drops in some evocative descriptions, like that
of dusk over the Exe estuary at the start of Chapter VI:

*A railway train flung a feather of steam to break the gloom afar off and
a gaggle of geese flew aloft, heard, but not seen. The shore did not reflect
this peace however, for the boats were sailing with the tide and not a few
fishermen stood up on the little breakwater with their dinghies waiting below.
The fishing fleet rode at anchor a quarter of a mile from the land. They were
set blackly on the still waters, and a boat or two from the haven had already
started for them. Women and landsmen stood about among the departing
fishers. Little groups talked, moved, mingled: lanterns twinkled and one by
one the shore boats carried their crews to sea.*

As mentioned **Eden Phillpotts** felt a keen sense of character in the local
landscape. In the process of setting its personality into literature, which he saw
as his duty as a writer, he also made sure to record the sound of its indigenous
speech, or in this case dialect. Part of his prodigious output involved a number of
poems and the following is one written in the Devon vernacular:

Man's Days

A sudden wakin', a sudden weepin';
A li'l suckin', a li'l sleepin';
A cheel's full joys an' a cheel's short sorrows,
Wi' a power o' faith in gert to-morrows.
Young blood red hot an' the love of a maid;
Wan glorious hour as'll never fade;

Some shadows, some sunshine, some triumphs, some tears;
An' a gatherin' weight o' the flyin' years.
Then auld man's talk o' the days behind 'e;
Your darter's youngest darter to min 'e;
A li'l dreamin', a li'l dyin',
A li'l lew corner o' airth to lie in.

Sowden Lane, Lympstone, one of the *'little streets'* down which *'ducks swim'* during the spring tides. See quote on page 130.

Pynes House, just below Upton Pyne village, overlooking the Exe valley. A strong contender for **Jane Austen**'s Barton Park in *Sense and Sensibility*.

15 UPTON PYNE

The area on the map demarked for East Devon District Council appears as a rough rectangle: one side sea, one side estuary and two land. However it possesses an anomaly, a strange, pointed fringe sprouting out of its top left hand corner directly above Exeter. But from the perspective of East Devon's literature, this must have been deliberate. For contained exactly within that fringe is the village of Upton Pyne, neatly positioned on a hilltop *'within four miles northward of Exeter.'* It is with these words that **Jane Austen** (1775-1817) identifies the setting of her first published novel, *Sense and Sensibility* (1811). Although her own hilltop village is called Barton and the centre of the book's action happens at the stately

134

home 'Barton Park,' Upton Pyne and particularly the William and Mary mansion, Pynes House below it, fit her descriptions surprisingly accurately. Looking for any alternatives within the four mile radius northward of Exeter, draws a total blank. It is known that Jane Austen preferred to write about places she knew and very likely that she would have spotted this elegant, pastoral location during one of her several trips down to Devon. Pynes House sits just above the Exe valley overlooked by one of the more attractive carriage routes into Exeter.

The book's heroines, Marianne and Elinor Dashwood, forced to abandon their large Sussex house for financial reasons, came to live in a cottage close to Barton Park, called Barton Cottage. Although much smaller than their former home, this was compensated for by cottage's setting and the East Devon view that *'gave them cheerfulness.'*

The *'large and handsome'* house at Barton Park was home of the Dashwood's relatives, the Middletons, *'who lived in a style of equal hospitality and elegance.'* As for the real Barton Cottage, one candidate may well be today's farm at Woodrow Barton, similarly positioned *'about half a mile'* from Pynes House. While the description of the cottage's architecture fails to fit the present building,

AUSTEN

135

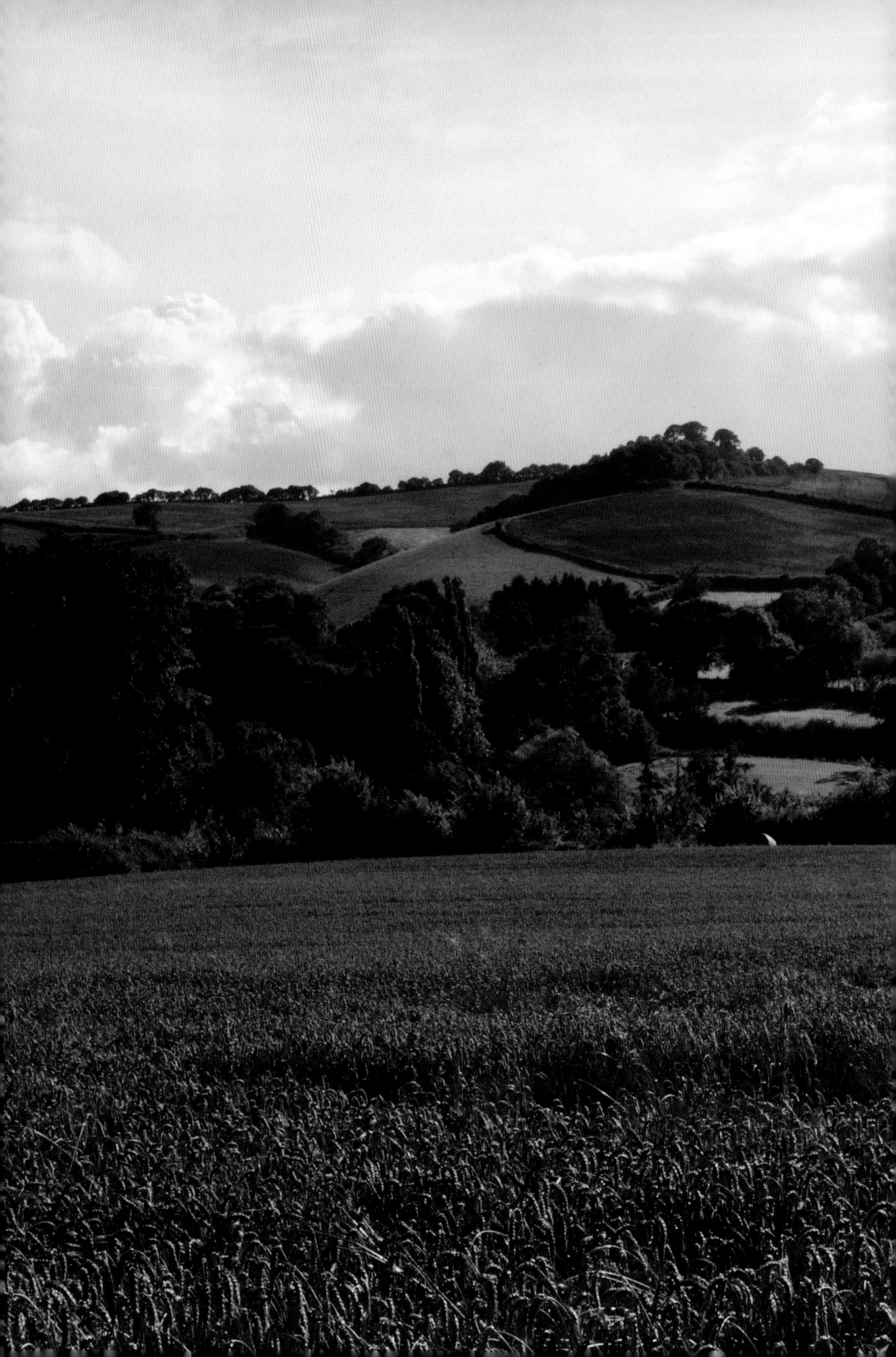

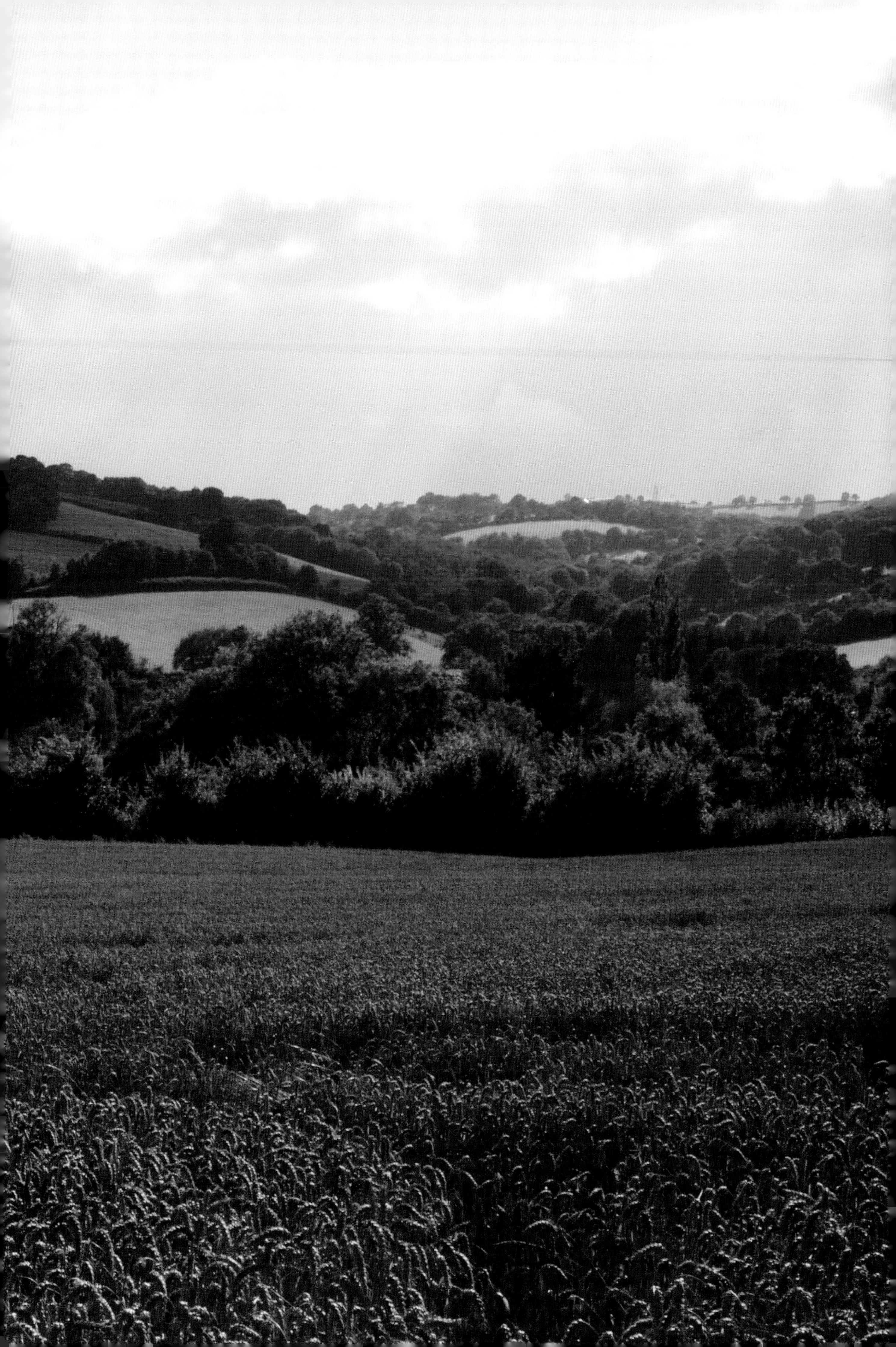

PREVIOUS PAGE
Hills rising before
the village of Upton
Pyne, close to the
beginning of **Walk
12;** see page 143.

Jane Austen as
drawn by the Up-
lyme artist Michael
Blooman.

the farm has undergone a major renovation since Austen's time. However it is
more the general setting of Barton village (Upton Pyne) and Barton Park (Pynes
House) that allows the comparison, as seen in the quote below from Chapter 6:

*The situation of the house was good. High hills rose immediately behind,
and at no great distance on each side; some of which were open downs, the
others cultivated and woody. The village of Barton was chiefly on one of these
hills, and formed a pleasant view from the cottage windows. The prospect in
front was more extensive; it commanded the whole of the valley, and reached
into the country beyond. The hills which surrounded the cottage terminated
the valley in that direction; under another name, and in another course, it
branched out again between two of the steepest of them.*

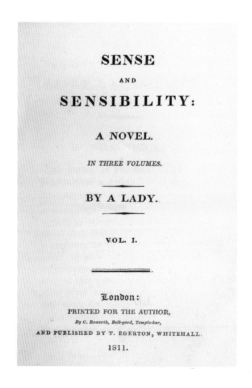

Title page of the origi-
nal edition of *Sense
and Sensibility,*
published in 1811.
Written by A Lady.

While the content of the landscape will have changed since the early 19th century, the shape and, more importantly, the feeling is very similar. Luckily this deeply rural section of the East Devon District Council area, close to the ever-expanding city of Exeter, remains undeveloped. For this reason the area still offers a number of superb walks very much in keeping with Jane Austen's observations from the novel's Chapter 9.

The whole country about them abounded in beautiful walks. The high downs which invited them from almost every window of the cottage to seek the exquisite enjoyment of air on their summits, were a happy alternative when the dirt of the valleys beneath shut up their superior beauties

Thus in the same spirit today a very pleasant walk can be taken by following the Exe Valley Way footpath eastwards from Cowley into what is almost certainly the Dashwood girls' East Devon homeland (for details see **Walk 12** on page 143). Passing beside Pynes House one can easily imagine the sisters strolling across the landscaped park in their crinoline and

Marianne, suddenly awakened by some accidental noise in the house, started hastily up; and with feverish wildness, cried out "Is mamma coming?"

bonnets, en route to dinner at Barton Park; or gazing anxiously out the windows waiting for a certain visitor. The grassy slope in front of Woodrow Barton farm also allows us to picture Marianne hurrying down, falling and spraining her ankle, which leads to the fateful encounter with John Willoughby.

The 1995, Academy Award-winning film of the book, starring Emma Thompson and Kate Winslet was shot elsewhere, leaving walkers along the

One of two images by William Greatbatch from the first illustrated edition of *Sense and Sensibility,* published in 1833. In it Elinor comforts her sick sister Marianne.

Exe Valley Way the privilege of knowing that they are discovering the real landscape as almost certainly envisioned by Jane Austen.

Before setting out, it might be worth reading the novel's Chapter 18 with its discussion of the 'picturesque,' as it is presented in the context of this piece of Devonshire landscape. Also it seems to satisfy both party's *idea[s] of a fine country.'* Some of the arguments in the extract below offer a good insight into her views on the popular admiration of nature, as well as to the Romantic movement itself, then in full flourish. In this section Marianne, who has been rhapsodising about the landscape around Barton Park, then asks Elinor's friend, Edward Ferrars for his thoughts. He replies:

"You must not enquire too far, Marianne—remember I have no knowledge in the picturesque, and I shall offend you by my ignorance and want of taste if we come to particulars. I shall call hills steep, which ought to be bold; surfaces strange and uncouth, which ought to be irregular and rugged; and distant objects out of sight, which ought only to be indistinct through the soft medium of a hazy atmosphere. You must be satisfied with such admiration as I can honestly give. I call it a very fine country—the hills are steep, the woods seem full of fine timber, and the valley looks comfortable and snug—with rich meadows and several neat farm houses scattered here and there. It exactly answers my idea of a fine country, because it unites beauty with utility—and I dare say it is a picturesque one too, because you admire it. I can easily believe

Woodrow Barton Farm. In location at least a possible contender for **Jane Austen's** Barton Cottage.

it to be full of rocks and promontories, grey moss and brush wood, but these are all lost on me. I know nothing of the picturesque."

"I am afraid it is but too true," said Marianne; "but why should you boast of it?"

"I suspect," said Elinor, "that to avoid one kind of affectation, Edward here falls into another. Because he believes many people pretend to more admiration of the beauties of nature than they really feel, and is disgusted with such pretensions, he affects greater indifference and less discrimination in viewing them himself than he possesses. He is fastidious and will have an affectation of his own."

"It is very true," said Marianne, "that admiration of landscape scenery is become a mere jargon. Everybody pretends to feel and tries to describe with the taste and elegance of him who first defined what picturesque beauty was. I detest jargon of every kind, and sometimes I have kept my feelings to myself, because I could find no language to describe them in but what was worn and hackneyed out of all sense and meaning."

"I am convinced," said Edward, "that you really feel all the delight in a fine prospect which you profess to feel. But, in return, your sister must allow me to feel no more than I profess. I like a fine prospect, but not on picturesque principles. I do not like crooked, twisted, blasted trees. I admire them much

View towards Stoke Woods and the river Exe from the living room of Woodrow Barton Farm.

AUSTEN

141

more if they are tall, straight, and flourishing. I do not like ruined, tattered cottages. I am not fond of nettles or thistles, or heath blossoms. I have more pleasure in a snug farm-house than a watch-tower—and a troop of tidy, happy villages please me better than the finest banditti in the world."

Stepping back from the specific points raised, it is worth recalling the school of thought that claims landscape itself can provide people with clues on how to act. This, it suggests, is why authors place certain characters into certain environments. Moving from one landscape into another is like shifting from one attitude to another, or casting a new emotional light onto one's life. The physical shape of hills or rivers, the arrangement of trees, the amount of sky, the prevailing weather, encourage subtle changes of behaviour. The mood of one piece of landscape is like someone whispering, chiding, pushing the character in a certain direction.

E.M. Forster, a great admirer of Jane Austen, once described her **Sanditon** (see page 86) as *'half topography, half romance,'* adding that in this more than any of her other novels *'topography comes to the front and is screwed much deeper than usual in to the story.'* (*Abinger Harvest* page 150). This kind of geographical plot is uncommon in **Jane Austen** whose novels are generally sparing in their use of natural description, as she prefers the psychological landscape. But it is always there, lurking quietly but solidly in the background. Just occasionally she breaks free and lets loose, as with her glowing description of Lyme Regis in **Persuasion,** (her last completed novel published in 1817 after her death), and especially its nearby Undercliff, (see page 44).

Sense and Sensibility's unique corner of Devon was carefully selected by the author, who travelled extensively around southern England. Standing on the hillock in front of Woodrow Barton Farm, looking out over the Exe valley one can easily imagine **Jane Austen**, the woman who described herself simply as 'A Lady' on the book's cover, sitting in a carriage on the turnpike, looking keenly out at this enchanted spot from the other direction. Was this not it; exactly the right spot for her Elinor and Marianne, with its perfect blend of beauty: utility and romanticism?

Today, thanks to the success of her novels, her presence has been fixed into this section of the Devon landscape and its hills imbided with her thoughts. But, as the Romantics might have responded, do they not also look keenly back at us?

Walk 12 - Jane Austen   The Exe valley

Pick up the Exe Valley Way walk at Cowley, on the A377 just north of Exeter. Cross the river Creedy following the B road until the entrance gates to Pynes House. Walk through and just after the gravel drive, find the path directly ahead. It follows the Exe valley, passes below what is almost certainly Jane Austen's Barton Park, giving a clear view of the estate parkland where the Dashwoods would have walked to be received by the ebullient Sir John Middleton. Half a mile further on the path bears left by Woodrow Barton farm (the strong contender for Barton Cottage). Beyond this another mile is Brampford Speke village. But just before the first house there is a chance to turn left onto the Devonshire Heartland Way which heads up the hill into Upton Pyne village itself. This allows the possibility of a circular route from the hilltop village, back down along the road to the start of the walk at the gates to Pynes House, or on the main road at Cowley.

Looking north towards the Exe valley from the top of Stoke Hill; a view the Dashwood sisters might have seen on one of their longer walks.

16 BROADCLYST

PHILLPOTTS

Driving up to a grand Victorian mansion, the home of a once prolific and famous writer, now largely forgotten, is a haunting experience. The red bricks of Kerswell House still stand as they did 65 years ago when serving as the writing chamber for **Eden Phillpotts** (1862-1960) – East Devon's most productive writer (for fuller details of his work see Chapter 14). From under those stone lintels, flowed 31 years' worth of hand-penned literature. The doorway would have opened to a host of renowned writers and thinkers, including the woman he mentored as a child, then promoted as a young writer, Agatha Christie. Indeed Christie said that Phillpott's fairy tale, **The Flint Heart,** remained the one she treasured above all others.

He would have ambled across that lawn with **Arthur Conan Doyle**, in whose writers' cricket team he occasionally played (see page 96); shared an after-dinner scotch with his friend Arnold Bennett or even **George Bernard Shaw** (see page 86). Back in his early days in London after he had launched his career, he collaborated on a play with Jerome K. Jerome (of *Three Men in a Boat* fame) which was then performed at the Lyric theatre. He also contributed regularly to Jerome's magazine, *The Idler*. But in 1899, unable to resist the call of his childhood home, he moved back to Devon where for the next 30 years he lived in Torquay, close to **Agatha Christie**'s house (she was 28 years his junior). Finally, in 1929, when 67, and at most people's retirement age, he transferred to his country fastness at Kerswell House, near Broadclyst. But he never stopped writing until, as his wife put it, his hand was unable to properly hold a pen. At this moment he promptly died, just two years shy of his hundredth birthday.

Looking at his house, one feels how the lives of writers are always such ghost-like events. Their product is a mere stream of words onto a page or screen, that once printed, can disappear so quickly and completely into a landscape, as Eden Phillpotts' have done. While Kerswell house stands so solidly, the nearby trees wave their branches back concerned with new, contemporary matters. The Exeter road just a few yards away, carries more cars whooshing past than ever before. The fields around it are disappearing at a speed never previously witnessed in Devon. A whole new world exists now and in it a town of 8,000 homes, Cranbrook, is being built just a few miles away. The tranquil landscape that welcomed this man of letters has departed, and today the position of this house would almost certainly not draw him in.

But while the words of Phillpotts the writer may have disappeared from the common mind, his actions, particularly as a campaigner, live on. Like most writers covered in this book, he had the vision to recognise the intrinsic value of countryside and do his best to save it from unnecessary development. During his tenure as President of the Dartmoor Preservation Association he was particularly active. The Association had many successes then and continues to build on them today. He added depth to his advocacy by explaining, through his 18 novels about Dartmoor, just why the area needed preserving. He did the same

Kerswell House, Broadclyst, the home of **Eden Phillpotts** for his last 31 years.

for East Devon with his novel **Redcliff,** about Lympstone and the Exe estuary (see Chapter 14). This is what a good writer can do, even if it means gently biting the hand that feeds it.

Amongst his many poems he wrote one called **Pixies' Plot.** In it he describes that place of wildness traditionally left in every Devonshire garden as a reservation for pixies. He would go on to describe Dartmoor as such, in relation to England.

Perhaps the last word should come from **Agatha Christie** herself who wrote the following passage about him in her 1977 autobiography. It concerned that crucial period in every young writer's life, just after finishing the first novel, when the mind fills with thoughts about whether to keep on going or simply abandon the dream and profession. Desperately needing advice but too shy to ask herself, she finally let her mother step in and make the appeal to their then famous neighbour:

Eden Phillpotts was an odd looking man, with a face more like a faun's than an ordinary human being's; an interesting face with its long eyes turned up at the corners… He hated social functions and hardly ever went out, in fact he hated seeing people… He was also fond of my mother who seldom bothered him with social invitations, but used to admire his garden and his many rare plants and shrubs. He said that of course he would read Agatha's literary attempt.

I can hardly express the gratitude I feel to him. He could so easily have uttered a few careless words of well-justified criticism and probably discouraged me for life. As it was he set out to help. He realised perfectly how shy I was and how difficult it was of me to speak of things. The letter he wrote contained very good advice.

'Some of the things you have written are capital. You have a great feeling for dialogue. You should stick to gay, natural dialogue. Try to cut all moralisations out of your novels; you are much too fond of them and nothing is more boring to read. Try to leave your characters alone, so that they speak for themselves, instead of always rushing in and telling them what to say, or to explain to the reader what they mean by what they are saying. That is for the reader to judge for himself…

Which is exactly what she went on to do; and since then millions of readers have done their own judging. As for the effects of that letter, no one will probably ever know.

The SEA ITSELF

For the final word on the literature and landscape of East Devon, it seems only appropriate to return to the place that attracted the great majority of its writers - the sea. This ever-changing landscape of so many shades of light, colour, atmosphere, also possesses that vital ingredient - infinite open space - into which writers love to gaze. As has been hinted, the feeling of a piece of landscape seems to transfer spontaneously into the unconscious mind. The sea most of the time, makes no demands on its observers. Its canvas is invigoratingly blank and the imagination can run free across it, as we have seen in these pages.

In this spirit and as a final gesture, we might join the contemporary poet **Harry Guest** (1928-) in this very process. The following poem was composed while walking along East Devon's magnificent red cliff tops, inhaling the atmosphere of the waves and mist below. It is a strong message of encouragement for others to come and do exctly the same - and so help preserve it.

GUEST

Coast Sonnet

I need the open spaces to compose -
a moor, a mountain-top, a cliff-path by
a thorn-set hedgerow with a single rose
listening to what the sea's not saying. Why
should what one does lack weight within the world
unless you massacre a millionaire,
fly cryptic flags not meant to be unfurled
or find a recipe to make despair
shrink like a blob of water in the sun?
The strand below lies between scarlet caves
and mild incoming tide. No quicksand. Should
the rain hold off nothing will scrape the waves
but zephyrs gently. There's no call for gun
or arrow back in the enchanted wood.
(February 2014)

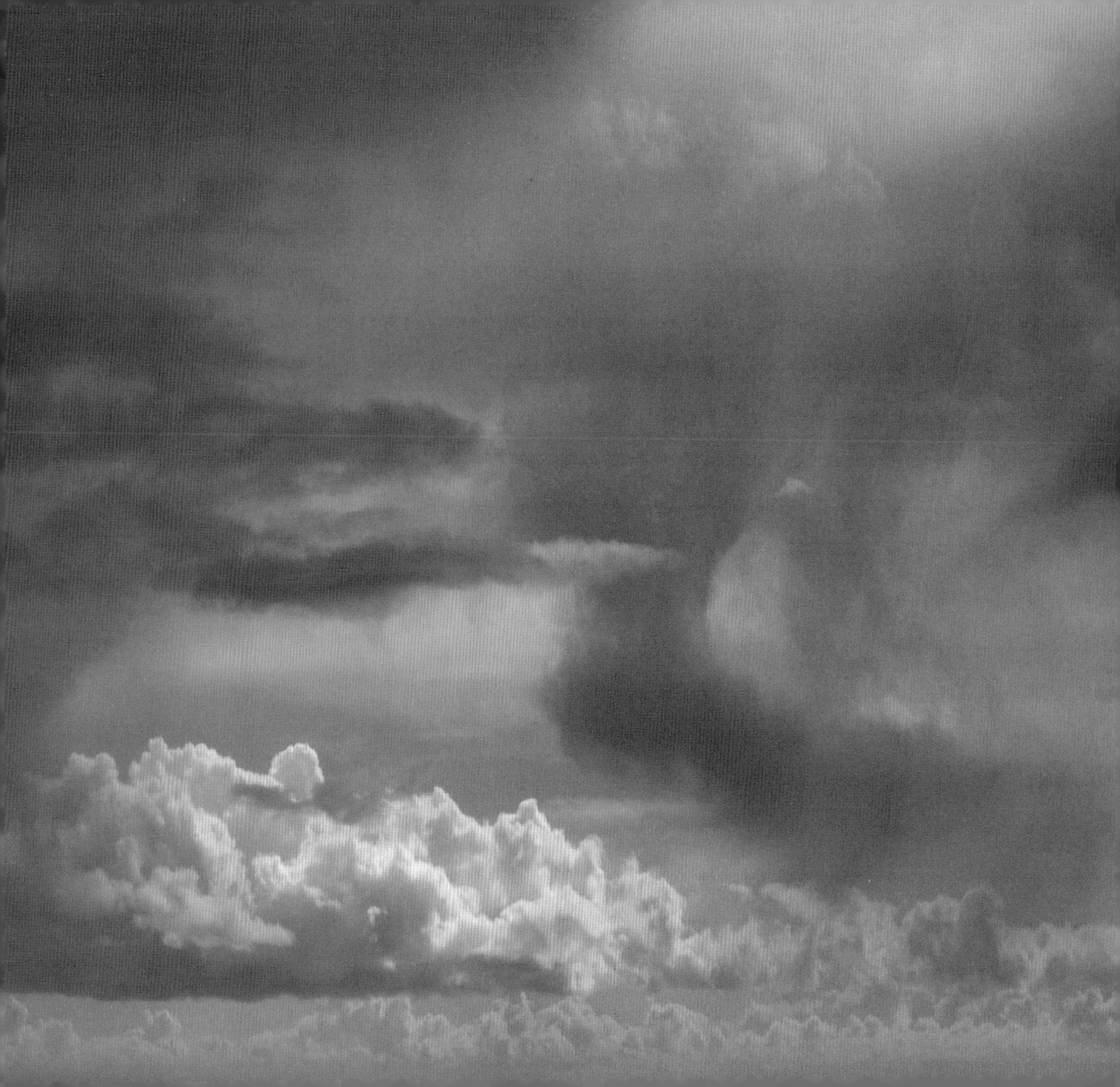

SELECT BIBLIOGRAPHY

Austen, Jane *Persuasion* John Murray 1818
Austen, Jane *Sanditon and other stories* Alfred Knopf 1996
Austen, Jane *Sense and Sensibility* T. Egerton 1811

Baring Gould, Rev Sabine *Devonshire Characters and Strange Events* Bodley Head 1908
Baring Gould, Rev Sabine *Winefred; A Story of the Chalk Cliffs* Methuen 1900
Baring Gould, Rev Sabine *Songs and Ballads of the West* Methuen 1891
Barrett (Browning), Elizabeth *The Seraphim and Other Poems* Saunders and Otley 1838
Beer, Patricia *Moon's Ottery* Hutchinson 1978
Beer, Patricia *Patricia Beer, Collected Poems* Carcanet Press 1988
Beer, Patricia *Mrs Beer's House* Macmillan 1968
Benson, Peter *The Other Occupant* Macmillan 1990
Betjeman, John *Betjeman's Britain* Folio Society 1999
Blackmore, R.D. *Perlycross, a tale of the western hills* Samson Low: Marston & Co 1894
Blake, Nicholas *The Smiler with the Knife* Collins 1939
Bradbrook M.C. *The School of Night* Cambridge University Press 1936
Bradbury, Richard *Riversmeet* The Muswell Press 2007
Brooke, Rupert *The Collected Poems of Rupert Brooke* John Lane Co 1915
Butler, Jeremy *Orlando Hutchinson's Travels in Victorian Devon* Devon Books 2000.

Coleridge, Samuel Taylor. *Rime of the Ancient Mariner* Illus Gustave Dore. Arcturus 2008
Conan Doyle Arthur *Micah Clarke* Thomas Nelson and Sons, London 1919
Conan Doyle Arthur *Memories and Adventures* Hodder and Stoughton 1924
Coxhead, J.J *Devon Traditions and Fairy-tales* Raleigh Press, Exmouth 1959
Christie, Agatha *Agatha Christie, an Autobiography* Collins 1977

Dayananda, James *Eden Phillpotts* University Press of America 1984
Day Lewis, Cecil *The Buried Day* Chattto and Windus 1960
Day Lewis, Cecil *A Time to Dance* Hogarth Press 1935
Day Lewis, Cecil *The Otterbury Incident* Putnam 1948
Defoe, Daniel *A Tour thro the Whole Island of Great Britain* London 1748
Delderfield, R.F *Bird's Eye View* Constable 1954
Delderfield, R.F *Farewell the Tranquil Mind* Werner Laurie, 1950
Delderfield, R.F *A Horseman Rides By* Hodder & Stoughton 1966
Delderfield, R.F *For My Own Amusement* Hodder & Stoughton 1968

Fort, Tom *The A303: highway to the sun* Simon & Schuster 2012
Forster, E.M *Abinger Harvest* Edward Arnold 1936
Fowles, John *The French Lieutenant's Woman* Jonathan Cape 1969
Fowles, John *The Magus, a revised version* Little Brown 1978
Fowles, John *Islands* Jonathan Cape 1978

Gardam, Jane *The Sidmouth Letters* Hamish Hamilton 1980
Godwin, Fay *LAND* Heinemann 1985
Gray, Todd *East Devon, Travellers' Tales* The Mint Press 2000

Guest, Harry *Some Times* Anvil Press 2010

Holmes, Richard *Coleridge, Early Visions* Hodder & Stoughton 1989
Hardy, Thomas *A Changed Man* Macmillan 1913
Hoskins, W.G *Devon* David and Charles, Newton Abbot 1972

Irvine, St John *Bernard Shaw, his Life, Work and Friends* Constable 1956

Kenyon, Frederic *The Letters of Elizabeth Barrett Browning* Smith, Elder & Co 1897

Lacey, Robert *Sir Water Raleigh* Weidenfeld and Nicolson 1973
Leland, John *The Itinerary of John Leland the Antiquary* Oxford 1710
Linder, Leslie *A History of the Writings of Beatrix Potter* Frederick Warne & Co 1971
Lindsey-Noble, Marion *R.F. Delderfield, Butterfly Moments* Cashmere Publishing 2007
Lister, Keith *Half My Life. The Story of Sabine Baring-Gould and Grace* Charnwood 2002
Long, Christopher *Exmouth Through Time* Amberley Publishing 2010

Mantel, Hilary *Wolf Hall* Fourth Estate, 2009
Molony, Rowland *Practising to Go* (with John Torrance) Hooken Press 2011
Morrall, Clare *The Man Who Disappeared* Paragon 2010

Pevsner, Nikolaus *South Devon* Penguin 1952
Phillpotts, Eden *From the Angle of 88* Hutchinson 1951
Phillpotts, Eden *Redcliff* Hutchinson and Co, London 1924
Potter, Beatrix *The Tale of Little Pig Robinson* Frederick Warne & Co, 1930
Potter, Beatrix *The Tale of Peter Rabbit* Frederick Warne & Co, 1901

Raleigh, Walter, Sir *The Poems of Sir Walter Raleigh* Longman 1814
Read, Mike *Forever England: The Life of Rupert Brooke* Mainstream 1997
Reynolds, Stephen *A Poor Man's House* John Lane 1908
Rowling, J.K *Harry Potter and the Goblet of Fire* Bloomsbury 2000
Rowling, J.K *Harry Potter and the Deathly Hallows* Bloomsbury 2007

Sherbourne, Michael *H.G. Wells, Another Kind of Life* Peter Owen 2010
Swete, Rev John *Travels in Georgian Devon* Devon Books 2000

Tennyson, *Alfred Ballads and other Poems* Kegan Paul & Co 1880
Thackeray, William Makepeace *Pendennis* Bradbury and Evans 1849/50
Thackeray, William Makepeace *Vanity Fair* London 1849
Torrance, John *Poems* (with Rowland Molony) Hooken Press 2009
Trevor, William *The Children of Dynmouth* Bodley Head 1976

Warburton, Eileen *John Fowles, a Life in Two Worlds* Jonathan Cape 2004
Wells, H.G *Selected Short Stories* Penguin 1958
Witham, John *My Native Home* Coleridge Bookshop 1984

INDEX

R

S

T

U

V

W

ACKNOWLEDGEMENTS

One difference between a landscape and a human being is that they age very differently. Landscape appears to regenerate itself flawlessly, shrink, expand and possess an eternal youth. We are the ones who must cease, but hopefully leave behind a legacy worthy of our days as its guest. The writers covered here certainly did their bit. As for those who helped point to their endeavours:

First and foremost the hat must be doffed to Michael Temple for his strong commitment and campaigning spirit in trying preserve East Devon's splendid countryside and heritage. So many of the entries here were identified by him and he provided invaluable help in the book's creation, not to mention his work as theatrical impresario with the East Devon Writing performances. In the same vein follows Robert Crick and Sandra Semple, plus the indefatigable Jackie and Tony Green and Graham Cooper who helped with the map. Along with most of the writers mentioned in these pages, fellow spirits in the same endeavour are the founding fathers (and mothers) of the East Devon Alliance whose cause this book wholeheartedly endorses; the heroic Clare Wright to whom we and the countryside all owe a debt. Roger Giles for the same. Gratitude also goes to Kelvin Dent; Richard Eley; Marianne Rixson; Richard Thurlow and all those at the 'Save Our Sidmouth' campaign. Included too are the sharp eyes of Kate Hughes; Bob Symes, Rab and Chris Barnard, Peter Soper from Sidmouth Museum; David Tucker, Director of Lyme Regis Museum who follows in John Fowles' footsteps accompanied by the ever-cheerful Graham Davies. The same gratitude also extends to Alan Arthur of Exmouth Museum, Ray Girvan of the Devon History Society; Sarah Obermuller Bennett; John and Hilary Spurling; Graham and Jaqueline Ward; Jeremy and Anne Bradshaw Smith; Carol Ackroyd of the Budleigh Literary Festival; Caroline Lambard for her patience.

PERMISSIONS AND COPYRIGHT ACKNOWLEDGEMENTS

The images on pages 48, 69, 74, 75, and the photograph of R.F. Delderfield on page 119, are reproduced by the kind permission of Sidmouth Museum.
The images on pages 33, 36, 39, 42, and the b/w photograph of Uplyme Mill on page 56 are printed here with kind permission of Lyme Regis Museum.
The images on pages 118 and the W.J. Delderfield advertisement insert from the opposite page's brochure on page 119, are printed here with kind permission of Exmouth Museum.
The coloured drawing of Chit Rock by J.M.W. Turner on page 68 is reproduced courtesy of the Whitworth Gallery, The University of Manchester.
The watercolour by Orlando Hutchinson on page 83 is reproduced with kind permission of the Devon Record Office.
Particular thanks are given to Michael Blooman for his portrait of Jane Austen on page 138, and those in the map.
Patricia Beer's poems *Mist Over the Otter Valley; The Estuary* and *The Branch Line* (extract) are quoted with the kind permission of Carcanet Press - who also sell her books.
Cecil Day Lewis's poem *The Watching Post* appears with the kind permission of Peters, Fraser & Dunlop.

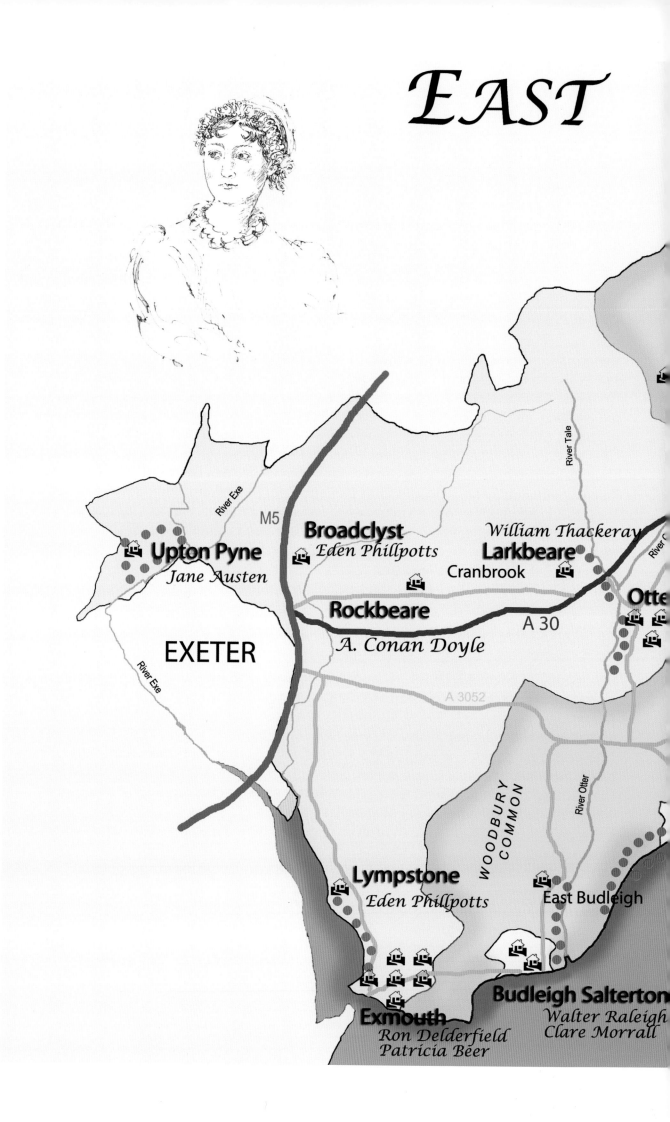

EAST

Upton Pyne
Jane Austen

Broadclyst
Eden Phillpotts

EXETER

Rockbeare
A. Conan Doyle

William Thackeray
Larkbeare
Cranbrook

M5

A 30

A 3052

River Exe

River Exe

River Tale

River Otter

WOODBURY COMMON

Ott

Lympstone
Eden Phillpotts

East Budleigh

Exmouth
Ron Delderfield
Patricia Beer

Budleigh Salterton
Walter Raleigh
Clare Morrall

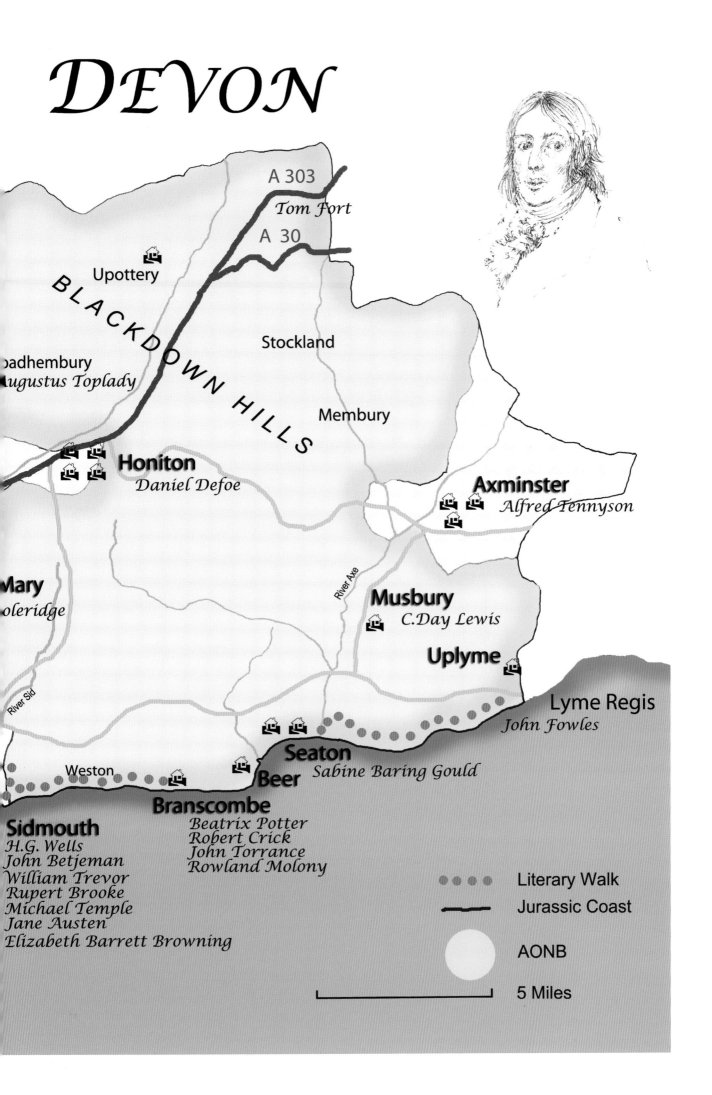

DEVON

A 303

Tom Fort

A 30

Upottery

BLACKDOWN HILLS

Stockland

Membury

Broadhembury
Augustus Toplady

Honiton
Daniel Defoe

Axminster
Alfred Tennyson

River Axe

Mary
Coleridge

Musbury
C. Day Lewis

Uplyme

River Sid

Lyme Regis
John Fowles

Seaton
Sabine Baring Gould

Weston

Beer

Branscombe

Sidmouth
H.G. Wells
John Betjeman
William Trevor
Rupert Brooke
Michael Temple
Jane Austen
Elizabeth Barrett Browning

Beatrix Potter
Robert Crick
John Torrance
Rowland Molony

● ● ● ● Literary Walk

━━━ Jurassic Coast

⬤ AONB

├─────────┤ 5 Miles

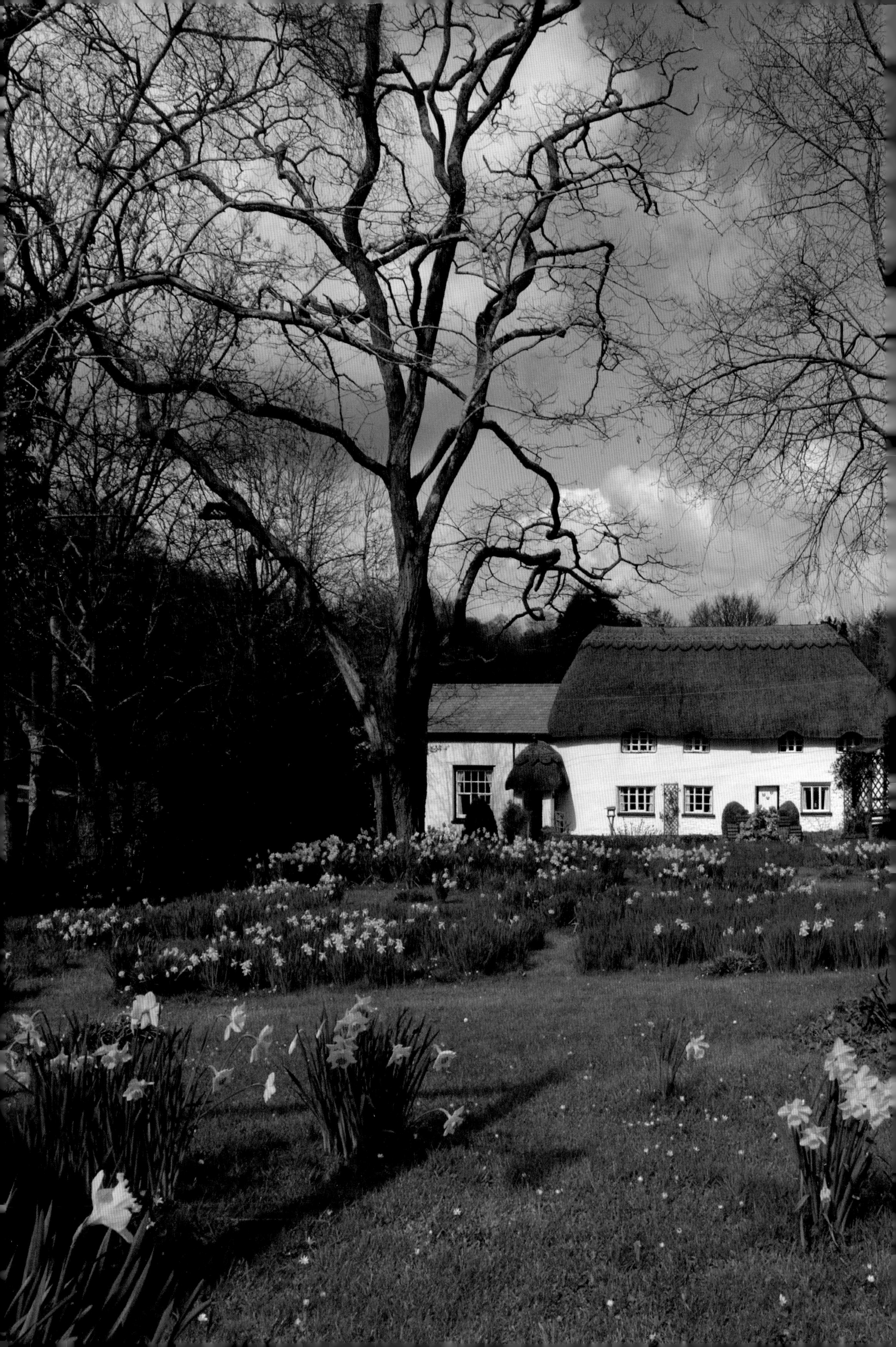

Published by

Mta Publications
27 Old Gloucester Street
LONDON WCIN 3AX

www.mtapublications.co.uk
email: inquiry@mtapublications.co.uk

In an association with
The
East Devon Alliance
www.eastdevonalliance.org

Pinn Cottage, (15th century) next to Harpford Wood, near Sidmouth.

Grasses in the hills above Sidbury

COVER PHOTO: Evening fog in Ladram Bay, near Sidmouth
BACK COVER PHOTO: Gittisham woods, near Honiton